big NATE

THUNKA, THUNKA, THUNKA

More

big NATE

adventures from

LINCOLN PEIRCE

Big Nate From the Top

Big Nate Out Loud

Big Nate and Friends

Big Nate Makes the Grade

Big Nate All Work and No Play

Big Nate: Game On!

Big Nate: I Can't Take It!

Big Nate: Great Minds Think Alike

Big Nate: The Crowd Goes Wild!

Big Nate's Greatest Hits

Big Nate: Say Good-bye to Dork City

Big Nate: Welcome to My World

big NATE
THUNKA, THUNKA, THUNKA

by LINCOLN PEIRCE

Andrews McMeel
Publishing®
a division of Andrews McMeel Universal

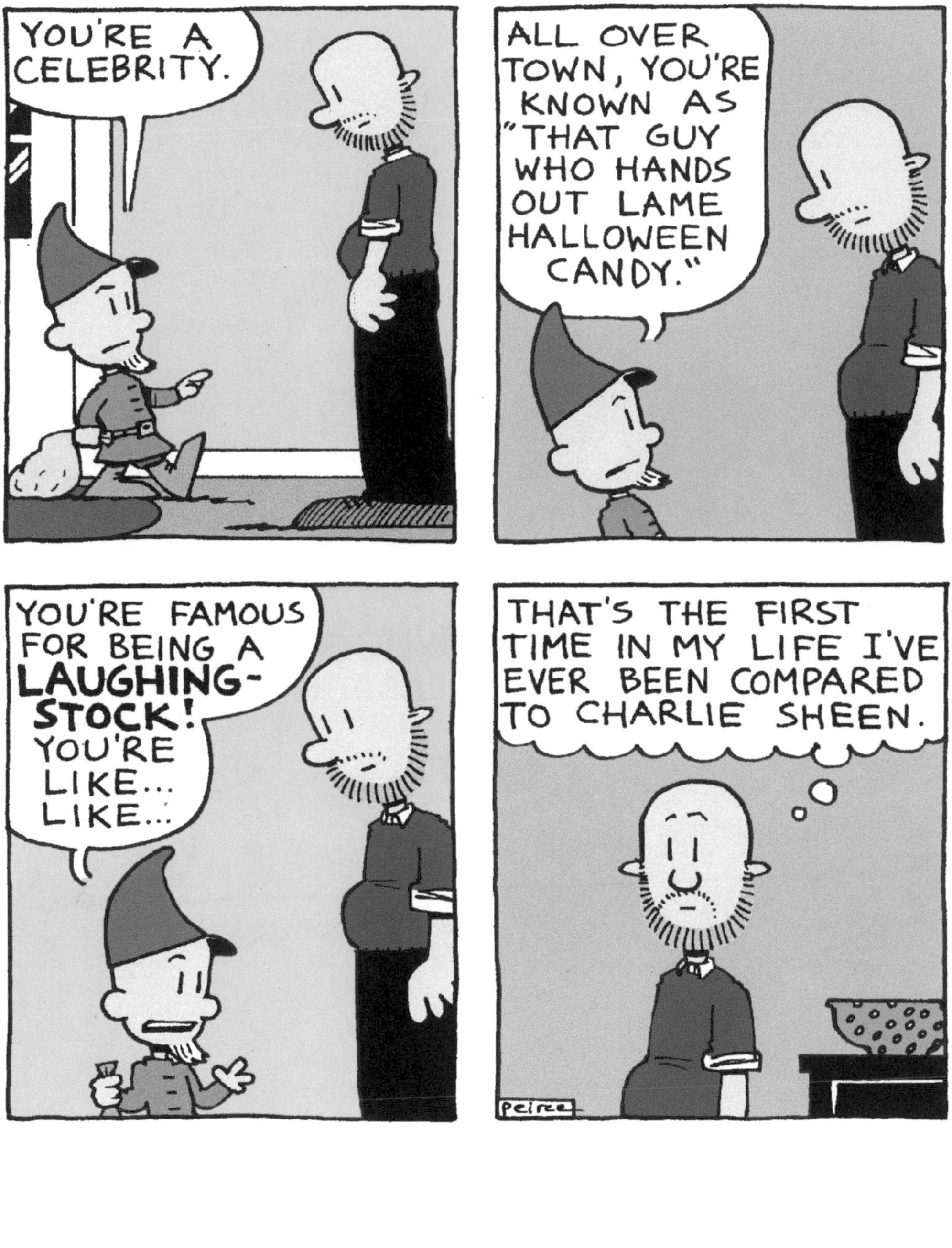
YOU'RE A CELEBRITY.
ALL OVER TOWN, YOU'RE KNOWN AS "THAT GUY WHO HANDS OUT LAME HALLOWEEN CANDY."
YOU'RE FAMOUS FOR BEING A **LAUGHING-STOCK!** YOU'RE LIKE... LIKE...
THAT'S THE FIRST TIME IN MY LIFE I'VE EVER BEEN COMPARED TO CHARLIE SHEEN.
peirce

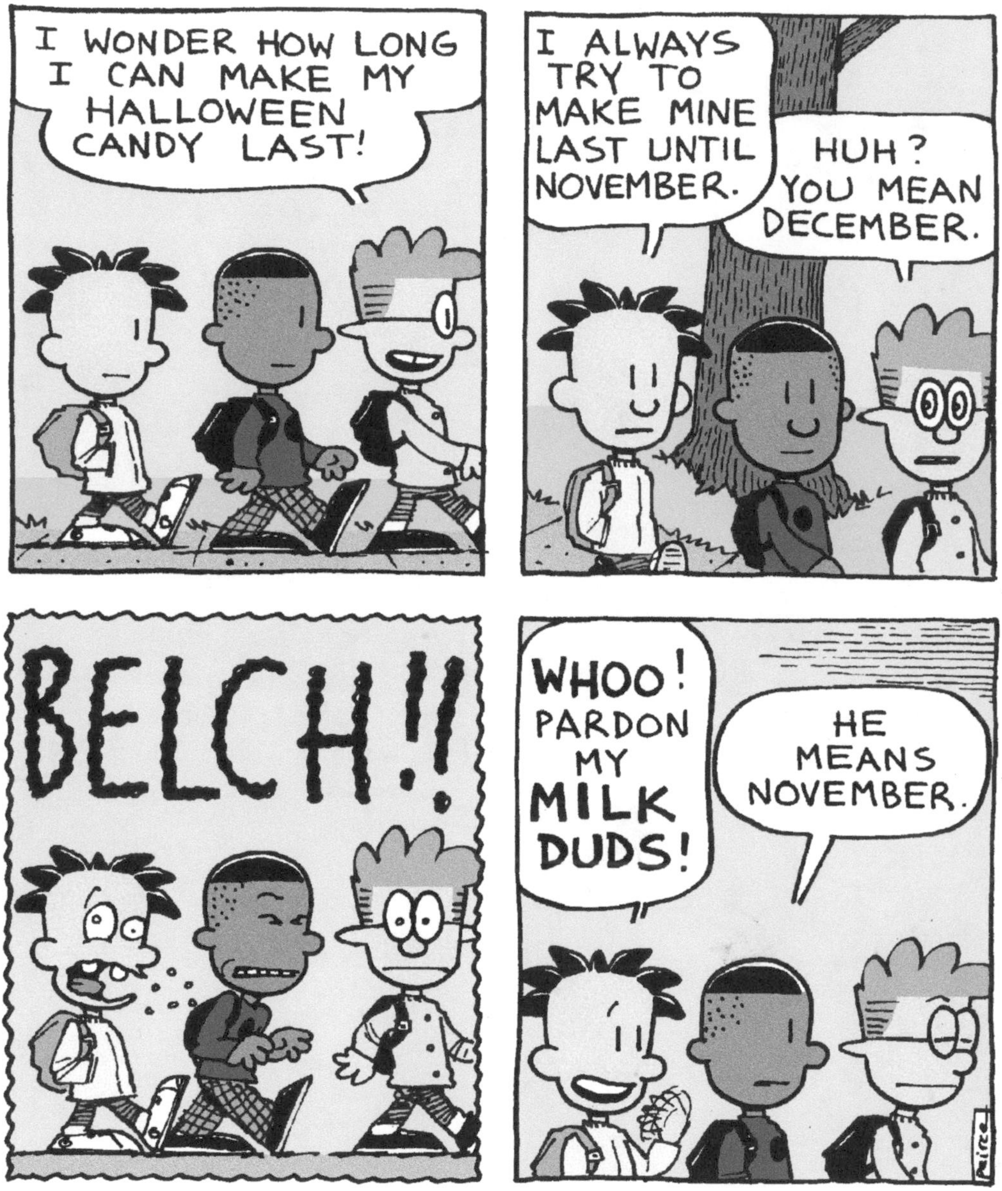
I WONDER HOW LONG I CAN MAKE MY HALLOWEEN CANDY LAST!
I ALWAYS TRY TO MAKE MINE LAST UNTIL NOVEMBER.
HUH? YOU MEAN DECEMBER.
BELCH!!
WHOO! PARDON MY MILK DUDS!
HE MEANS NOVEMBER.

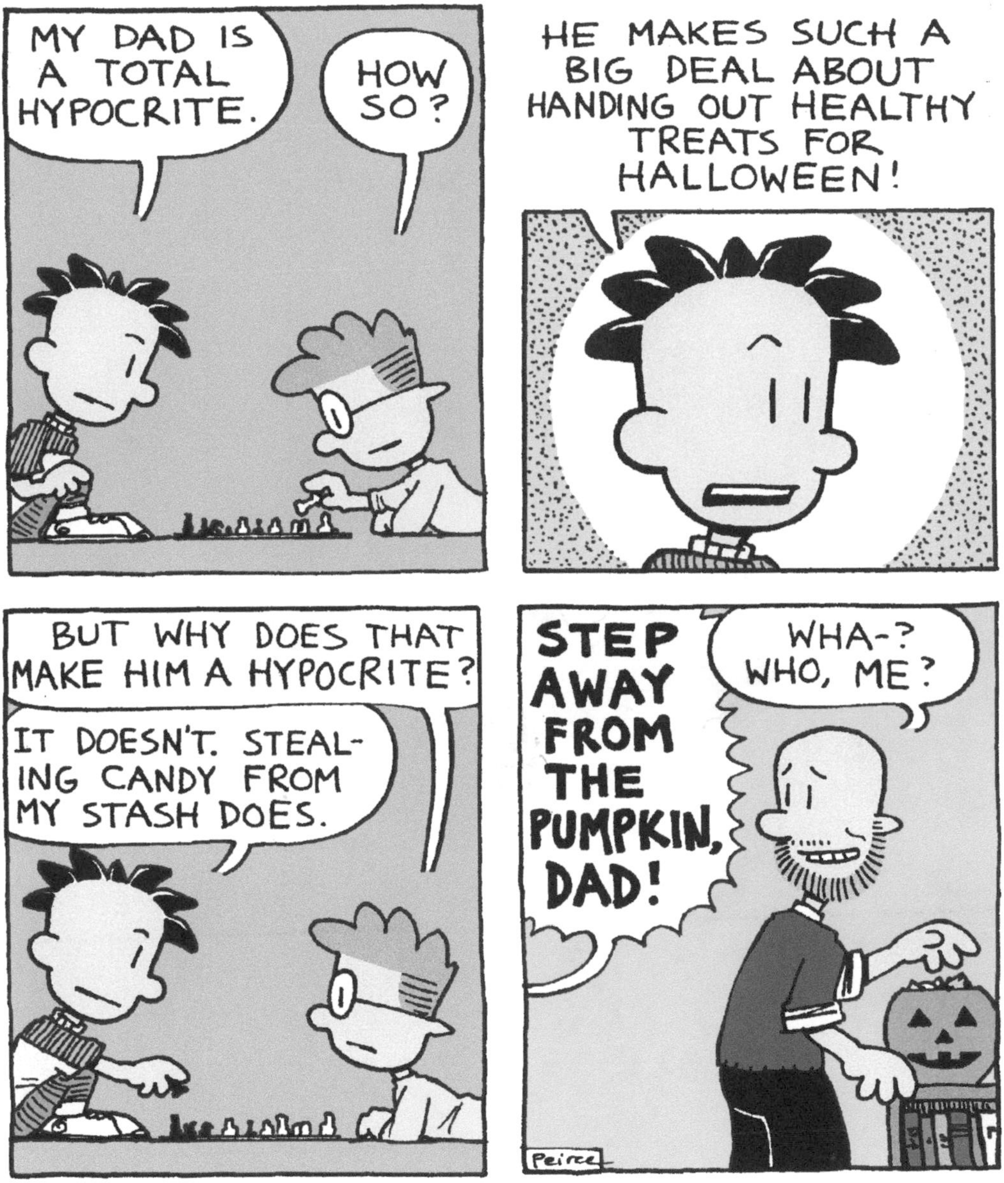
MY DAD IS A TOTAL HYPOCRITE.
HOW SO?
HE MAKES SUCH A BIG DEAL ABOUT HANDING OUT HEALTHY TREATS FOR HALLOWEEN!
BUT WHY DOES THAT MAKE HIM A HYPOCRITE?
IT DOESN'T. STEALING CANDY FROM MY STASH DOES.
STEP AWAY FROM THE PUMPKIN, DAD!
WHA-? WHO, ME?
Peirce

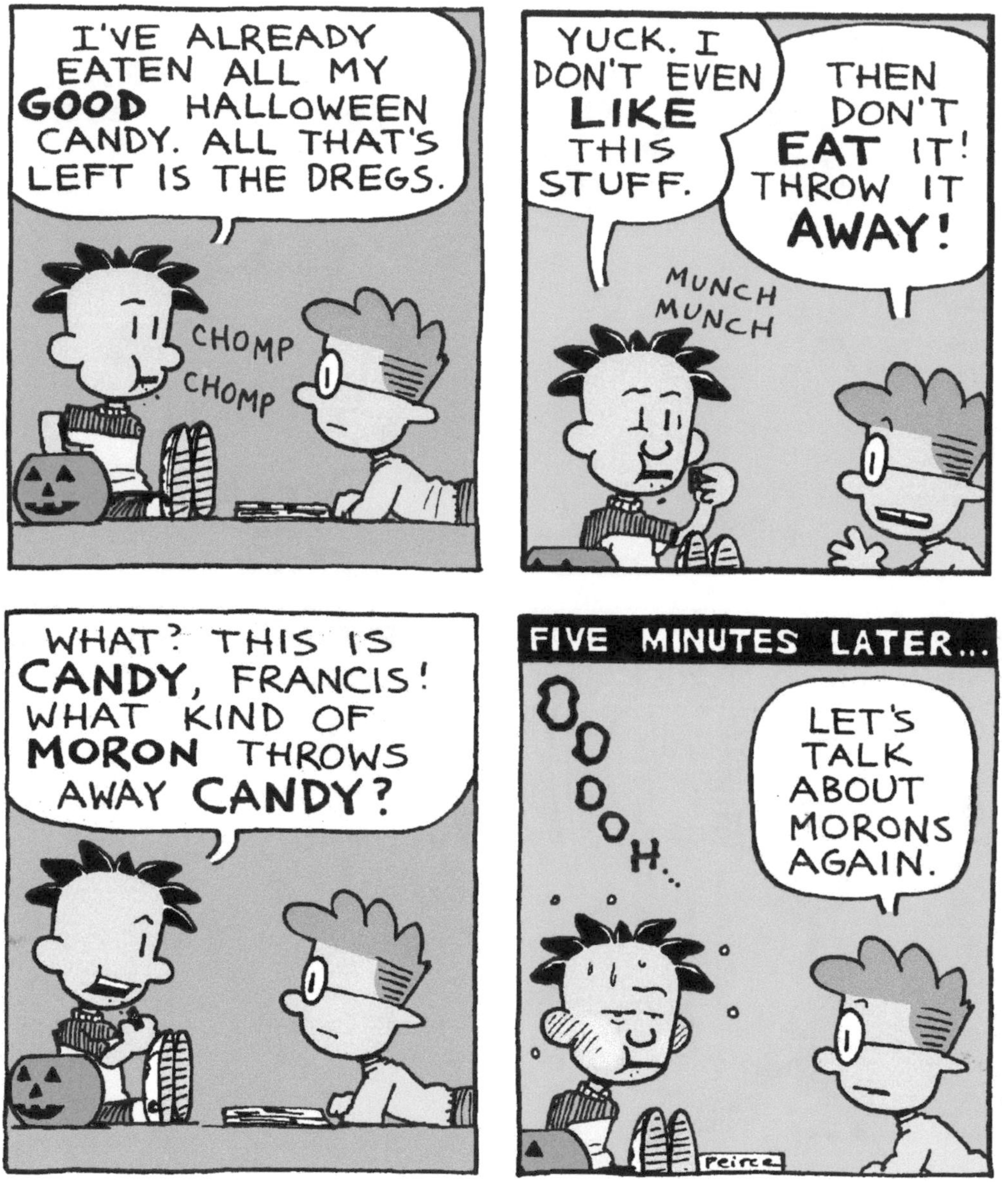
I'VE ALREADY EATEN ALL MY GOOD HALLOWEEN CANDY. ALL THAT'S LEFT IS THE DREGS.
CHOMP
CHOMP
YUCK. I DON'T EVEN LIKE THIS STUFF.
THEN DON'T EAT IT! THROW IT AWAY!
MUNCH
MUNCH
WHAT? THIS IS CANDY, FRANCIS! WHAT KIND OF MORON THROWS AWAY CANDY?
FIVE MINUTES LATER...
OOOOH...
LET'S TALK ABOUT MORONS AGAIN.
Peirce

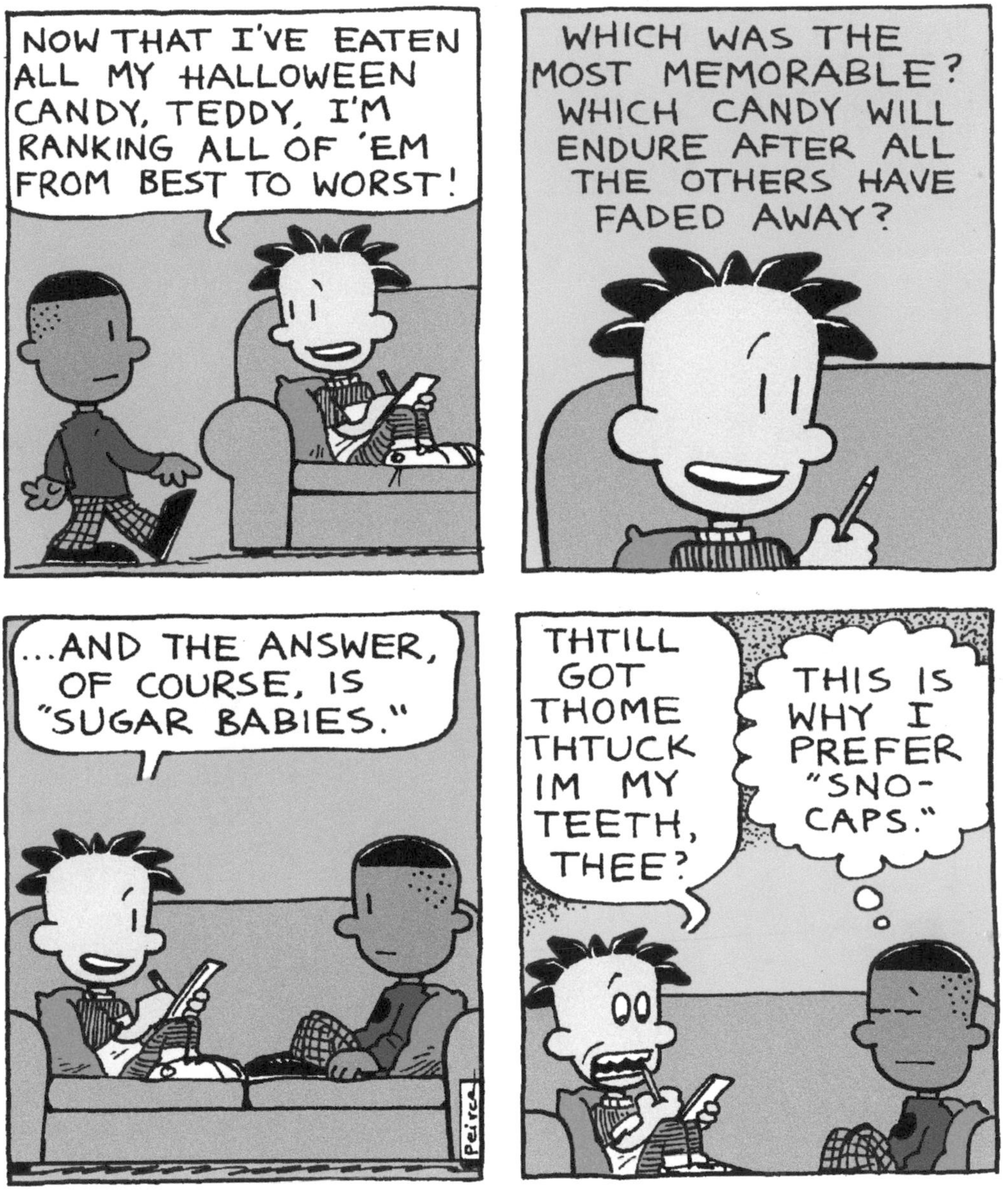
NOW THAT I'VE EATEN ALL MY HALLOWEEN CANDY, TEDDY, I'M RANKING ALL OF 'EM FROM BEST TO WORST!
WHICH WAS THE MOST MEMORABLE? WHICH CANDY WILL ENDURE AFTER ALL THE OTHERS HAVE FADED AWAY?
...AND THE ANSWER, OF COURSE, IS "SUGAR BABIES."
Peirce
THTILL GOT THOME THTUCK IM MY TEETH, THEE?
THIS IS WHY I PREFER "SNO-CAPS."

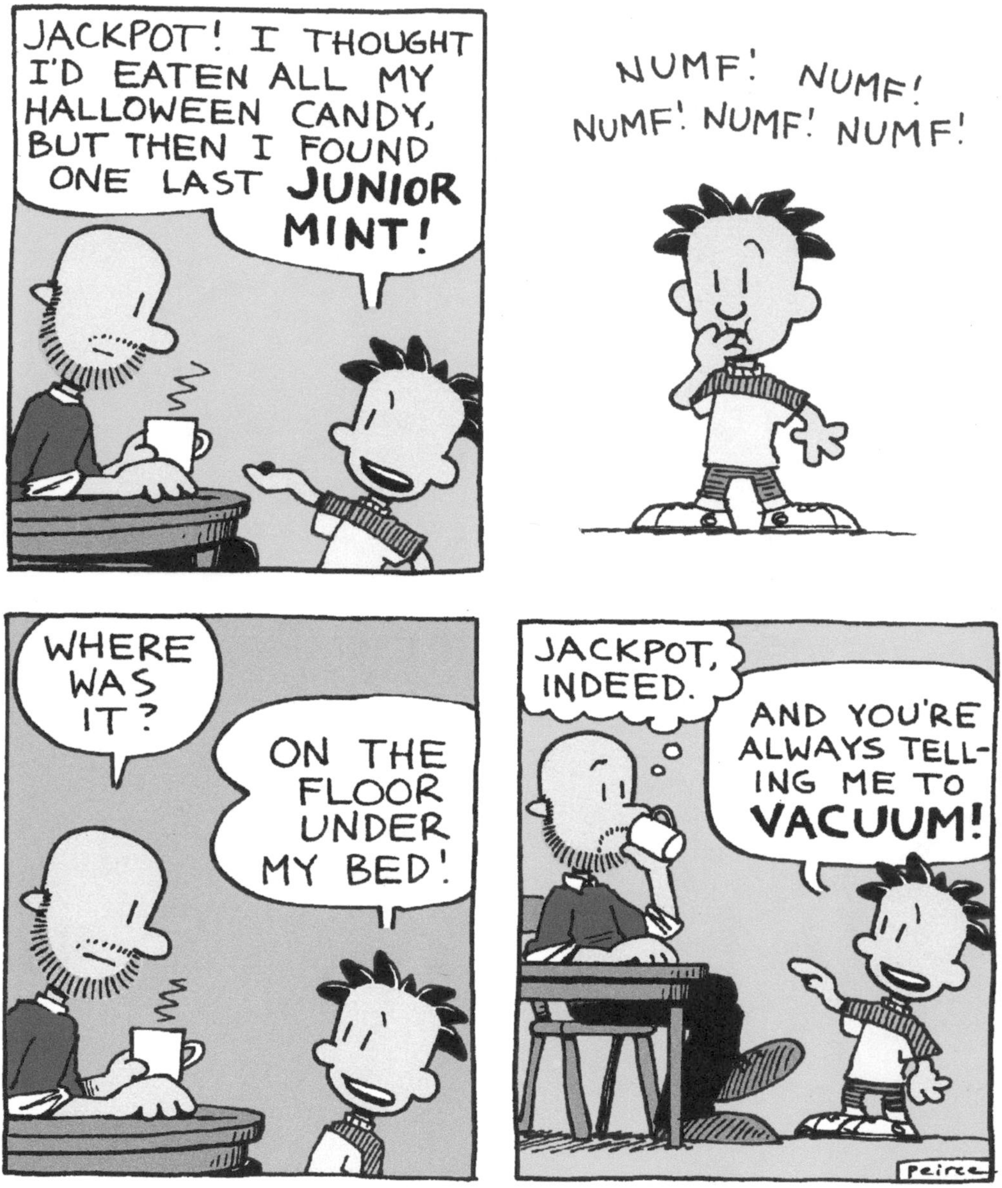
JACKPOT! I THOUGHT I'D EATEN ALL MY HALLOWEEN CANDY, BUT THEN I FOUND ONE LAST **JUNIOR MINT!**
NUMF! NUMF! NUMF! NUMF! NUMF!
WHERE WAS IT?
ON THE FLOOR UNDER MY BED!
JACKPOT, INDEED.
AND YOU'RE ALWAYS TELL-ING ME TO **VACUUM!**
Peirce

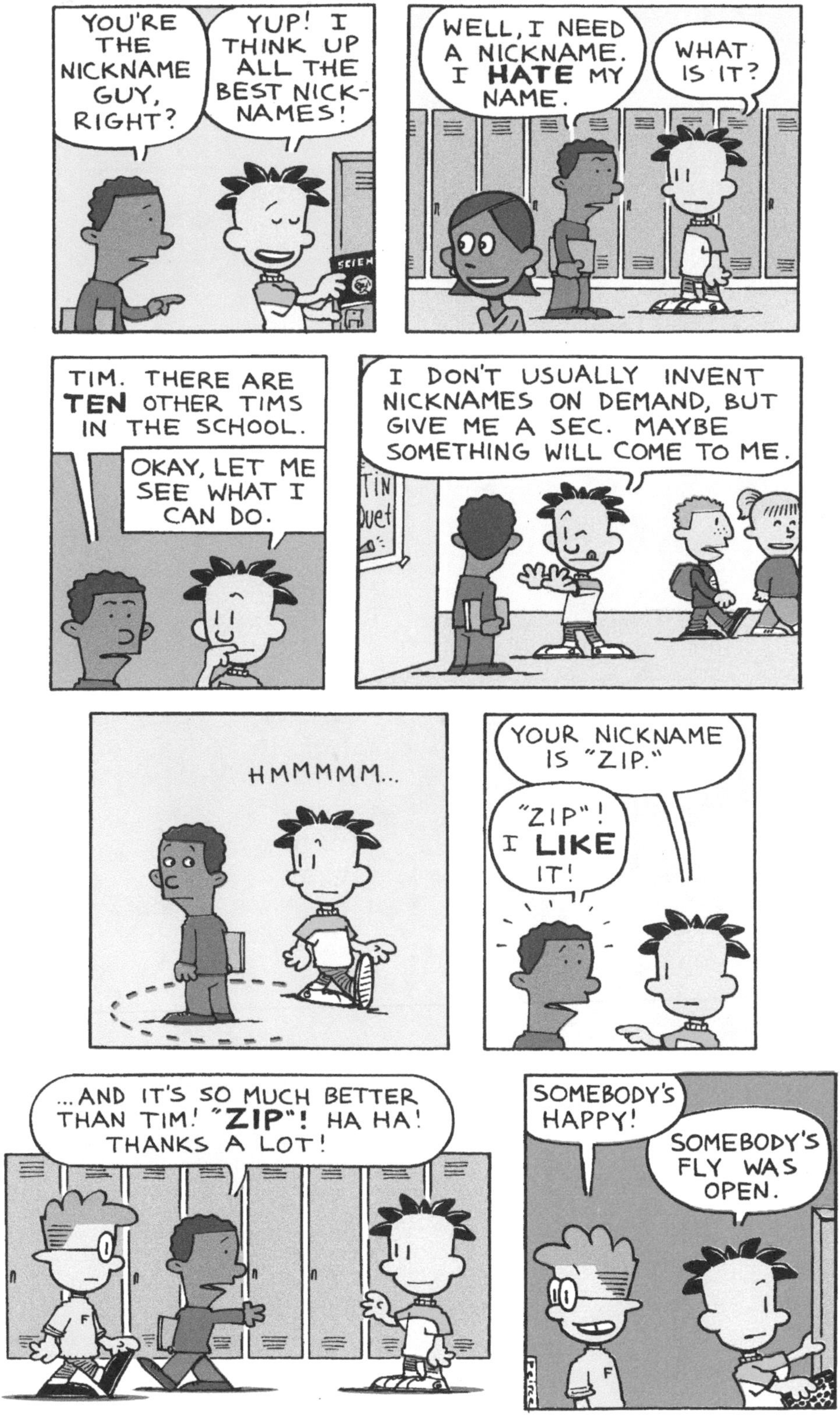
YOU'RE THE NICKNAME GUY, RIGHT?
YUP! I THINK UP ALL THE BEST NICK-NAMES!
WELL, I NEED A NICKNAME. I **HATE** MY NAME.
WHAT IS IT?
TIM. THERE ARE **TEN** OTHER TIMS IN THE SCHOOL.
OKAY, LET ME SEE WHAT I CAN DO.
I DON'T USUALLY INVENT NICKNAMES ON DEMAND, BUT GIVE ME A SEC. MAYBE SOMETHING WILL COME TO ME.
HMMMMM...
YOUR NICKNAME IS "ZIP."
"ZIP"! I **LIKE** IT!
...AND IT'S SO MUCH BETTER THAN TIM! **"ZIP"!** HA HA! THANKS A LOT!
SOMEBODY'S HAPPY!
SOMEBODY'S FLY WAS OPEN.

YOUR NEXT PROJECT WILL BE CONDUCTING AN INTERVIEW WITH A SENIOR CITIZEN!
WHAT'S THAT?
AN ELDERLY PERSON.
HOW OLD DO THEY HAVE TO BE?
LET'S SAY... SEVENTY.
WHAT IF SHE'S SEVENTY-FIVE BUT TELLS EVERY-ONE SHE'S SIXTY-SIX?
THAT'S FINE, CHAD.
Peirce

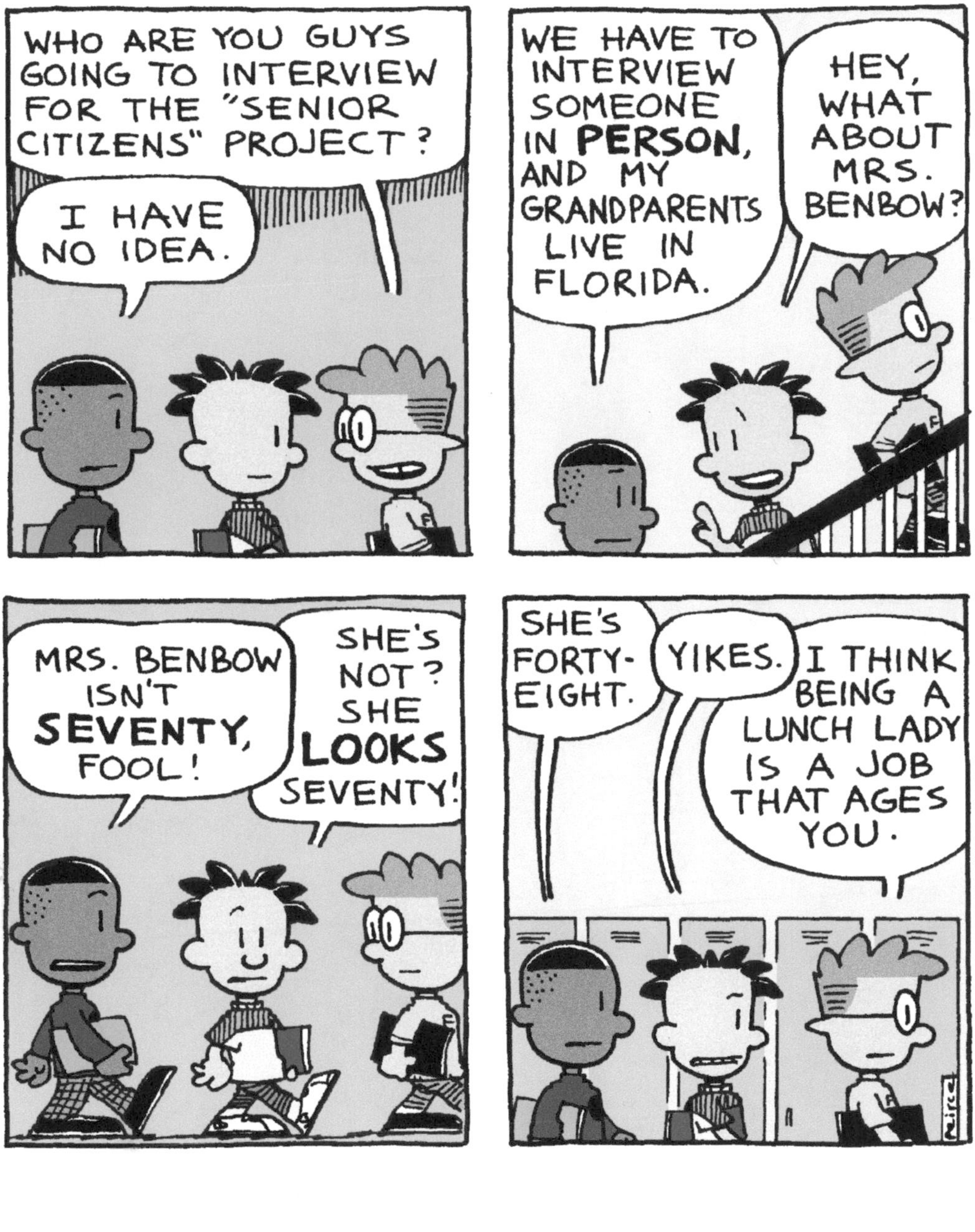
WHO ARE YOU GUYS GOING TO INTERVIEW FOR THE "SENIOR CITIZENS" PROJECT?
I HAVE NO IDEA.
WE HAVE TO INTERVIEW SOMEONE IN **PERSON**, AND MY GRANDPARENTS LIVE IN FLORIDA.
HEY, WHAT ABOUT MRS. BENBOW?
MRS. BENBOW ISN'T **SEVENTY**, FOOL!
SHE'S NOT? SHE **LOOKS** SEVENTY!
SHE'S FORTY-EIGHT.
YIKES.
I THINK BEING A LUNCH LADY IS A JOB THAT AGES YOU.
PEIRCE

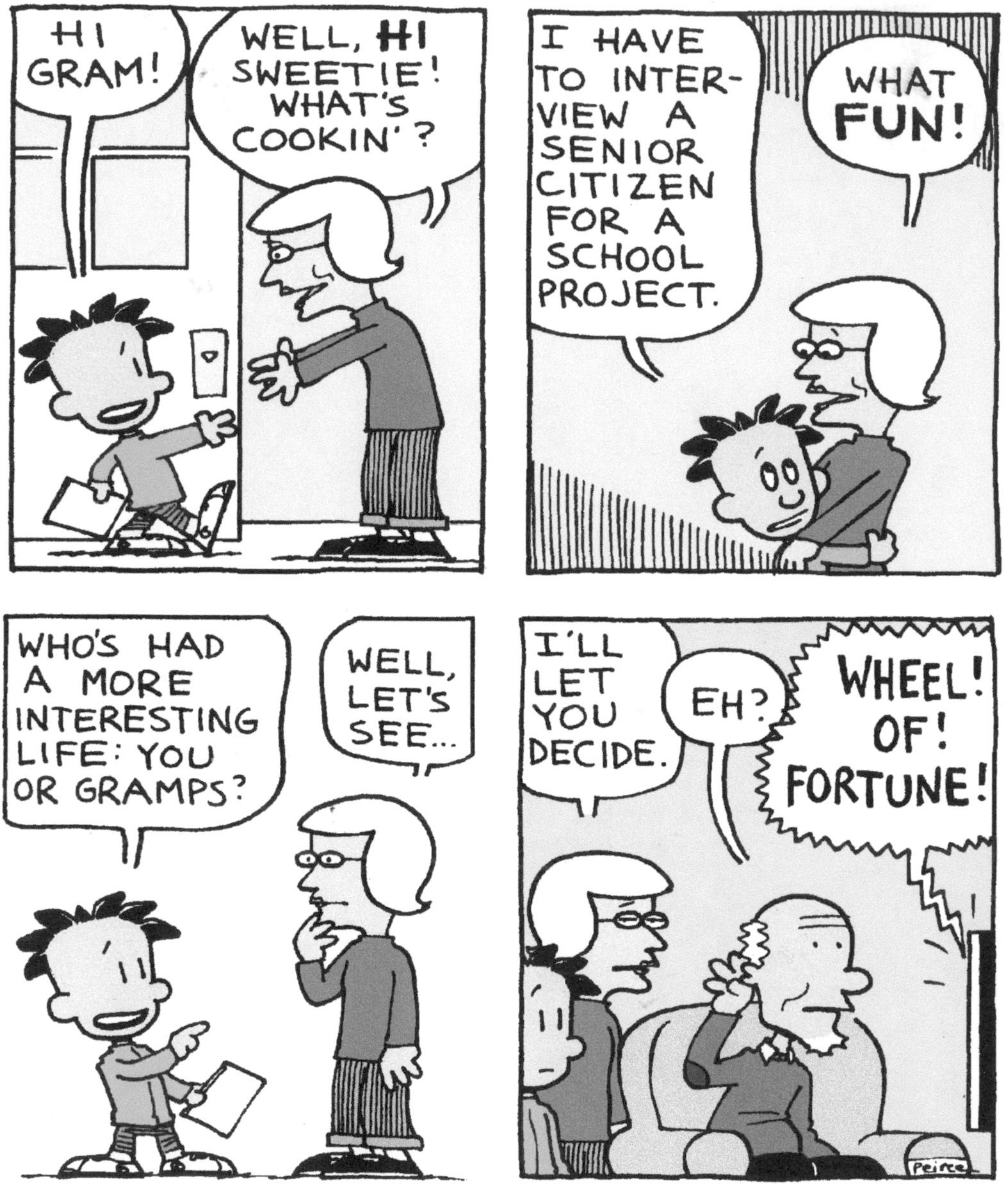
HI GRAM!
WELL, HI SWEETIE! WHAT'S COOKIN'?
I HAVE TO INTER-VIEW A SENIOR CITIZEN FOR A SCHOOL PROJECT.
WHAT FUN!
WHO'S HAD A MORE INTERESTING LIFE: YOU OR GRAMPS?
WELL, LET'S SEE...
I'LL LET YOU DECIDE.
EH?
WHEEL! OF! FORTUNE!
Peirce

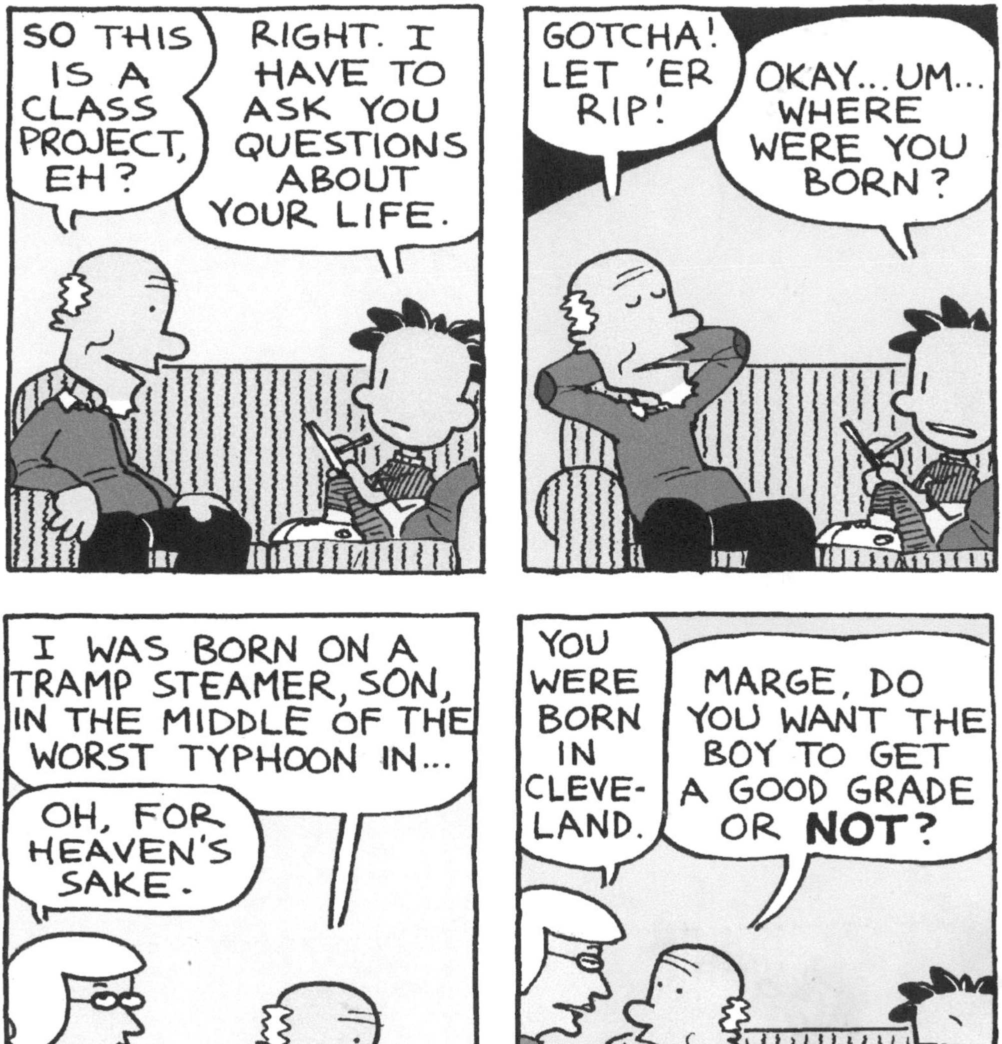

SO THIS IS A CLASS PROJECT, EH?
RIGHT. I HAVE TO ASK YOU QUESTIONS ABOUT YOUR LIFE.
GOTCHA! LET 'ER RIP!
OKAY... UM... WHERE WERE YOU BORN?
I WAS BORN ON A TRAMP STEAMER, SON, IN THE MIDDLE OF THE WORST TYPHOON IN...
OH, FOR HEAVEN'S SAKE.
YOU WERE BORN IN CLEVE-LAND.
MARGE, DO YOU WANT THE BOY TO GET A GOOD GRADE OR **NOT**?

OKAY GRAMPS, NEXT QUESTION: WHAT DO YOU REMEMBER MOST ABOUT YOUR CHILDHOOD?

WORK, M'BOY! WORK!

MY DAD ALWAYS HAD CHORES FOR ME TO DO! CHOPPING WOOD! SHOVELING SNOW! WEEDING THE GARDEN!

I TELL YOU, I WAS ONE HARD-WORKING KID! I'VE **ALWAYS** BEEN HARD-WORKING!

...AND YET, SOMEHOW, HE CAN'T MANAGE TO PICK HIS BOXERS UP OFF THE FLOOR.

YES, MARGE.

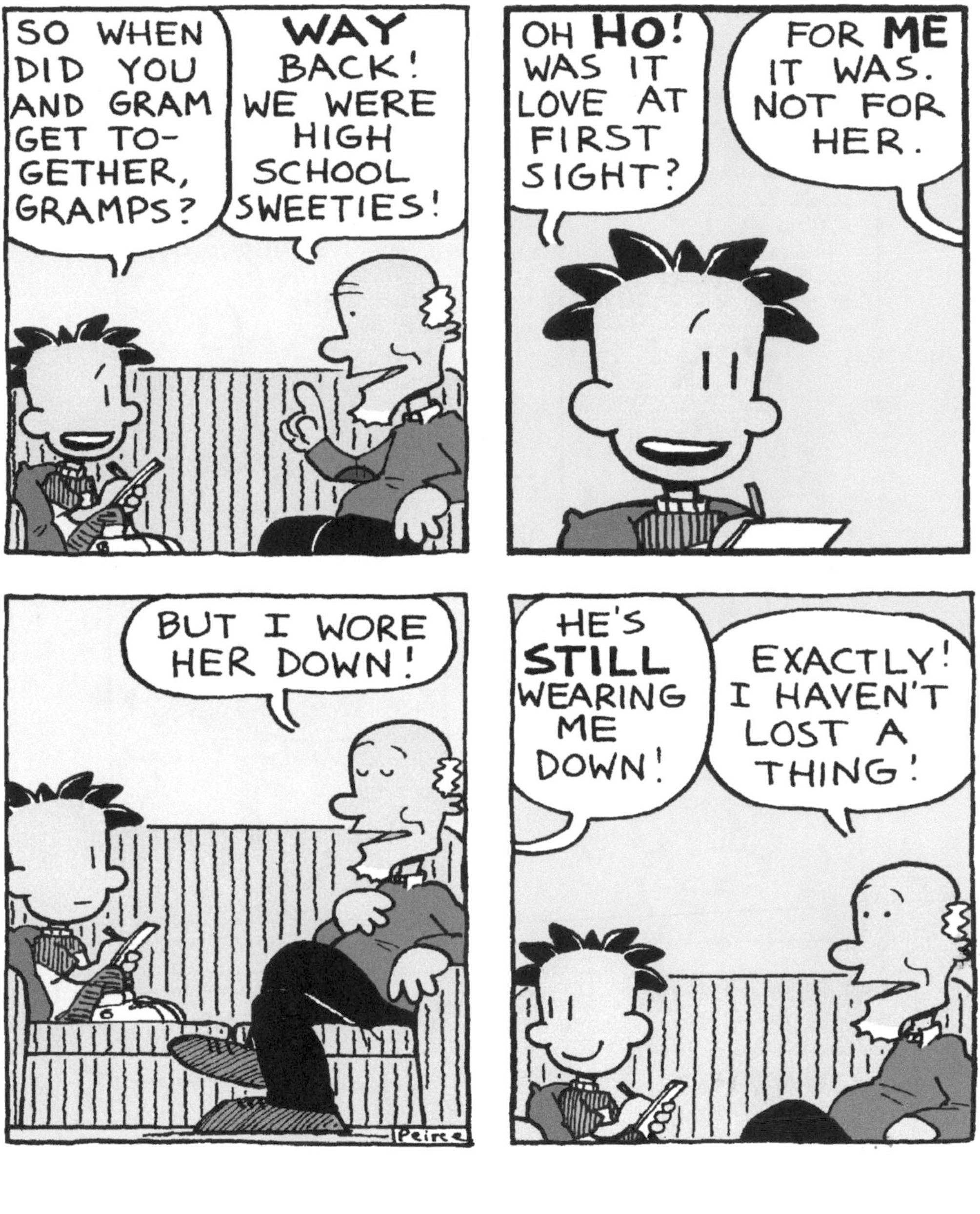
SO WHEN DID YOU AND GRAM GET TOGETHER, GRAMPS?
WAY BACK! WE WERE HIGH SCHOOL SWEETIES!
OH HO! WAS IT LOVE AT FIRST SIGHT?
FOR ME IT WAS. NOT FOR HER.
BUT I WORE HER DOWN!
Peirce
HE'S STILL WEARING ME DOWN!
EXACTLY! I HAVEN'T LOST A THING!

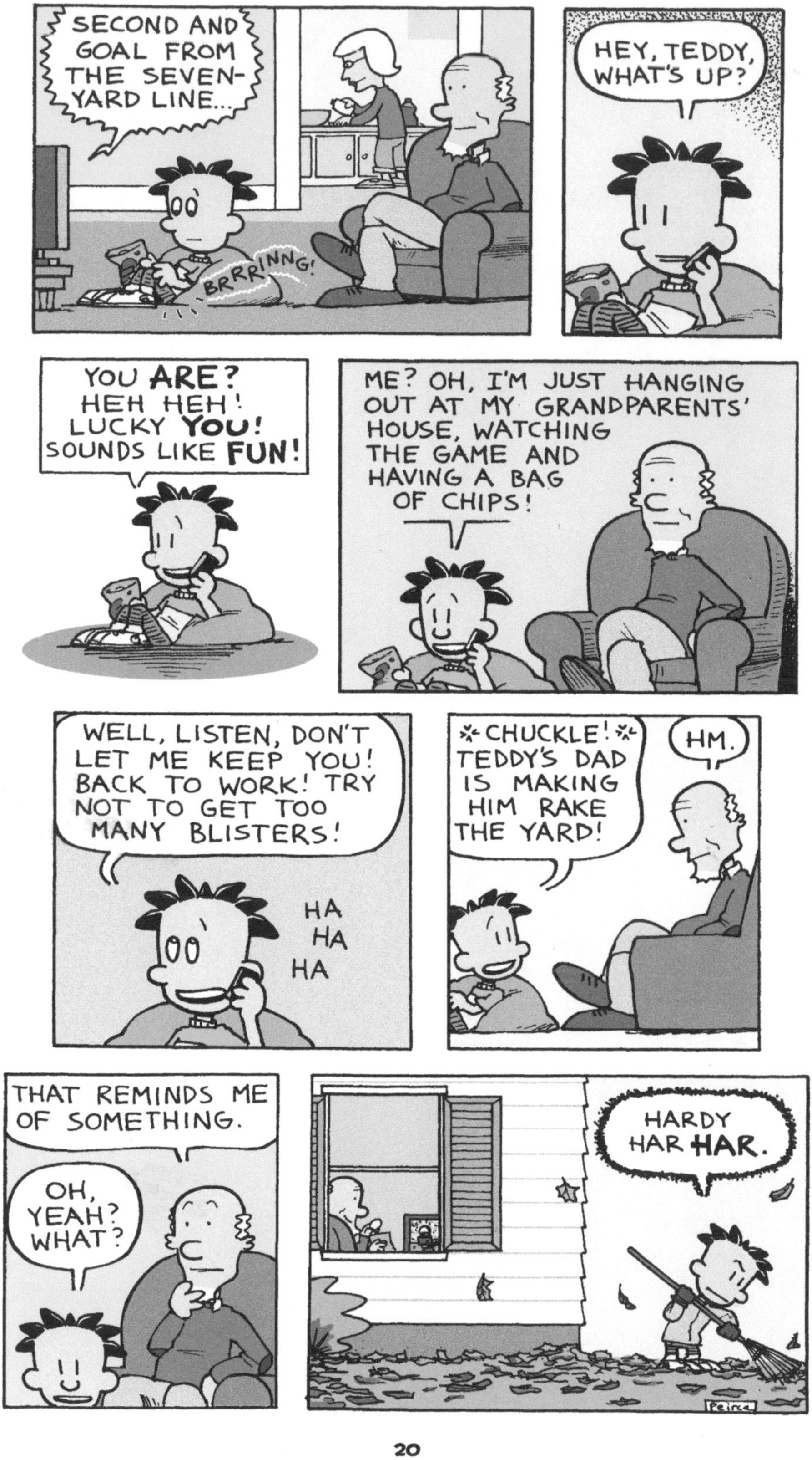
SECOND AND GOAL FROM THE SEVEN-YARD LINE...
BRRRINNG!
HEY, TEDDY, WHAT'S UP?
YOU ARE? HEH HEH! LUCKY YOU! SOUNDS LIKE FUN!
ME? OH, I'M JUST HANGING OUT AT MY GRANDPARENTS' HOUSE, WATCHING THE GAME AND HAVING A BAG OF CHIPS!
WELL, LISTEN, DON'T LET ME KEEP YOU! BACK TO WORK! TRY NOT TO GET TOO MANY BLISTERS!
HA HA HA
CHUCKLE! TEDDY'S DAD IS MAKING HIM RAKE THE YARD!
HM.
THAT REMINDS ME OF SOMETHING.
OH, YEAH? WHAT?
HARDY HAR HAR.
Peirce

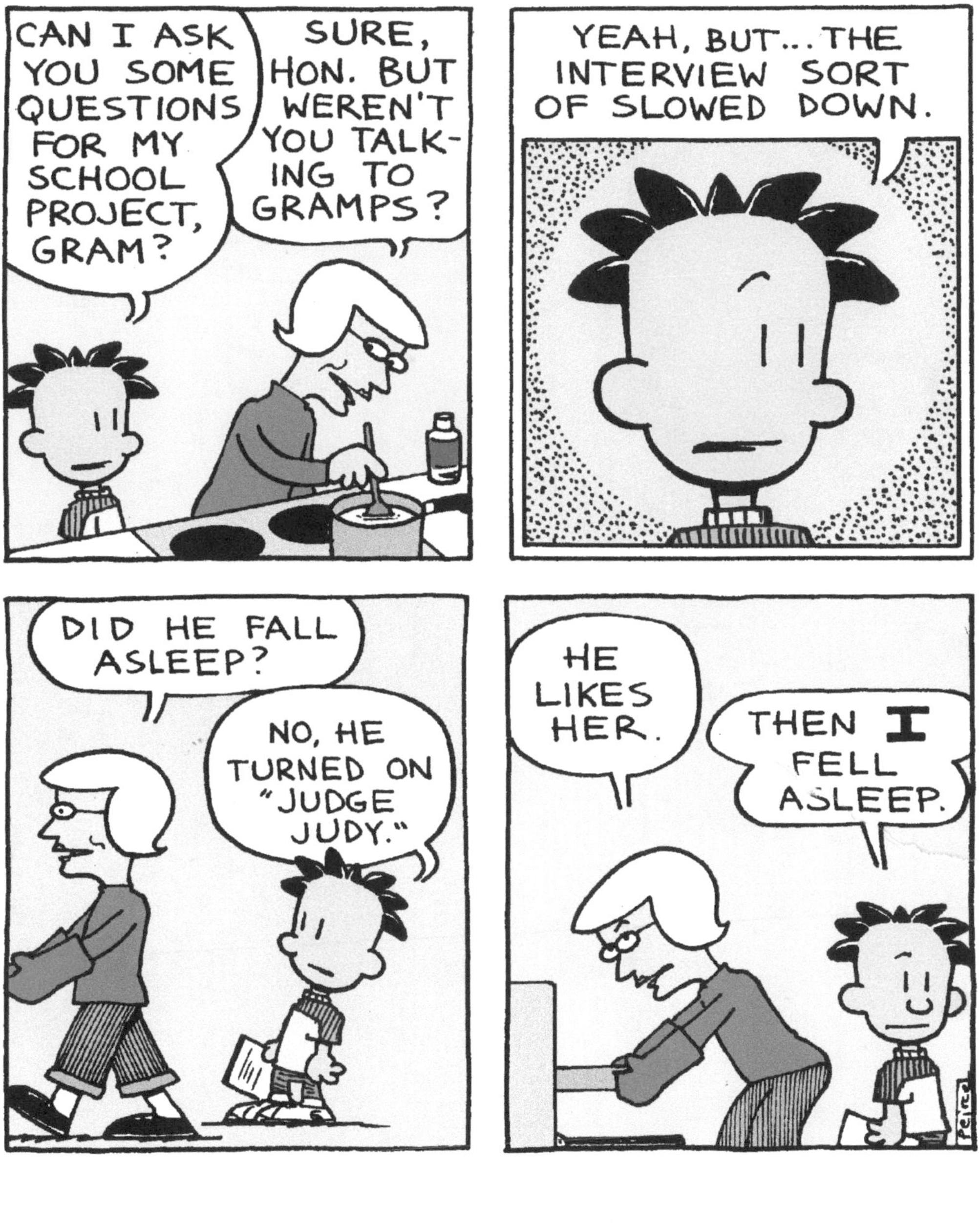

CAN I ASK YOU SOME QUESTIONS FOR MY SCHOOL PROJECT, GRAM?
SURE, HON. BUT WEREN'T YOU TALKING TO GRAMPS?
YEAH, BUT... THE INTERVIEW SORT OF SLOWED DOWN.
DID HE FALL ASLEEP?
NO, HE TURNED ON "JUDGE JUDY."
HE LIKES HER.
THEN I FELL ASLEEP.
PEIRCE

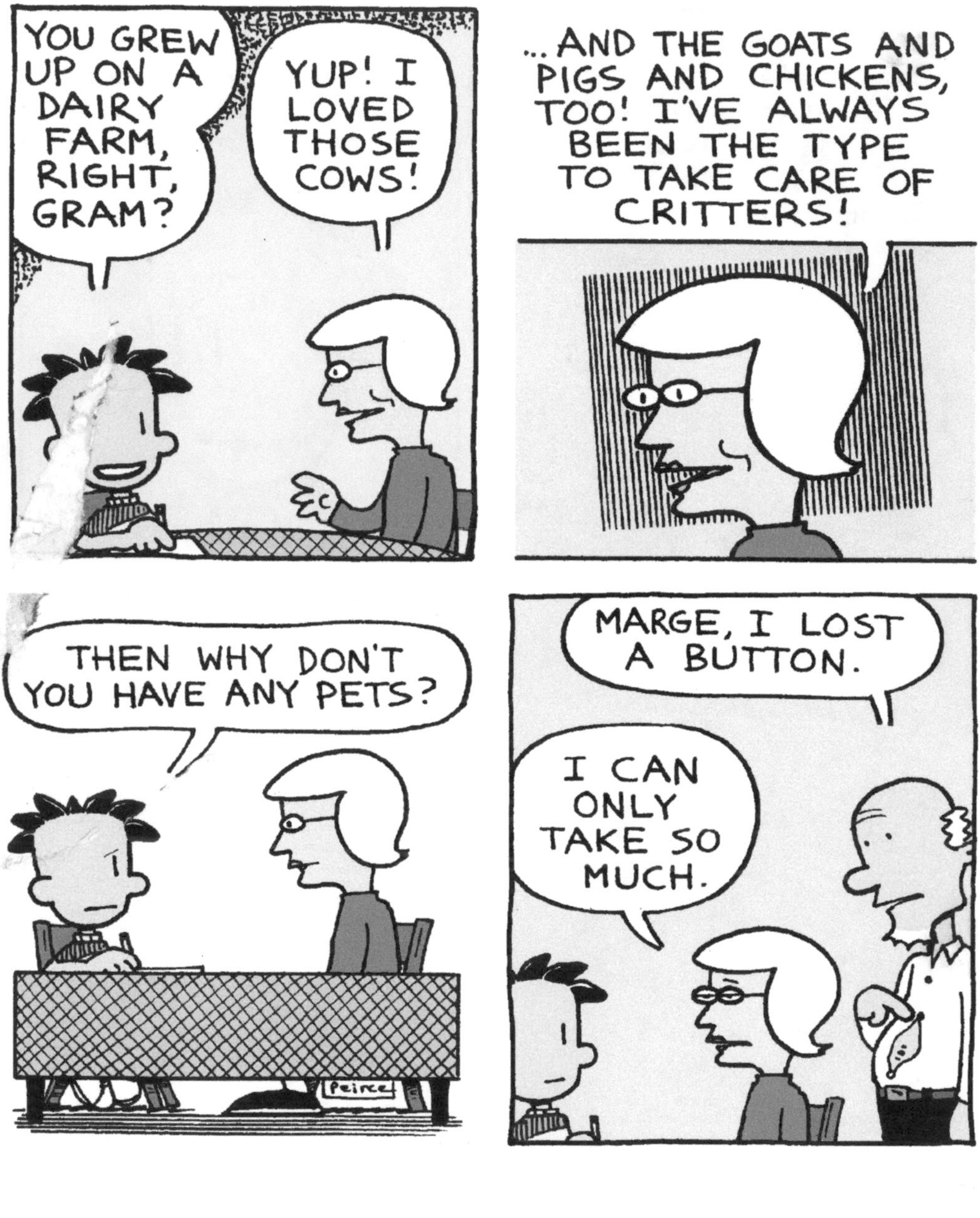
YOU GREW UP ON A DAIRY FARM, RIGHT, GRAM?
YUP! I LOVED THOSE COWS!
...AND THE GOATS AND PIGS AND CHICKENS, TOO! I'VE ALWAYS BEEN THE TYPE TO TAKE CARE OF CRITTERS!
THEN WHY DON'T YOU HAVE ANY PETS?
Peirce
MARGE, I LOST A BUTTON.
I CAN ONLY TAKE SO MUCH.

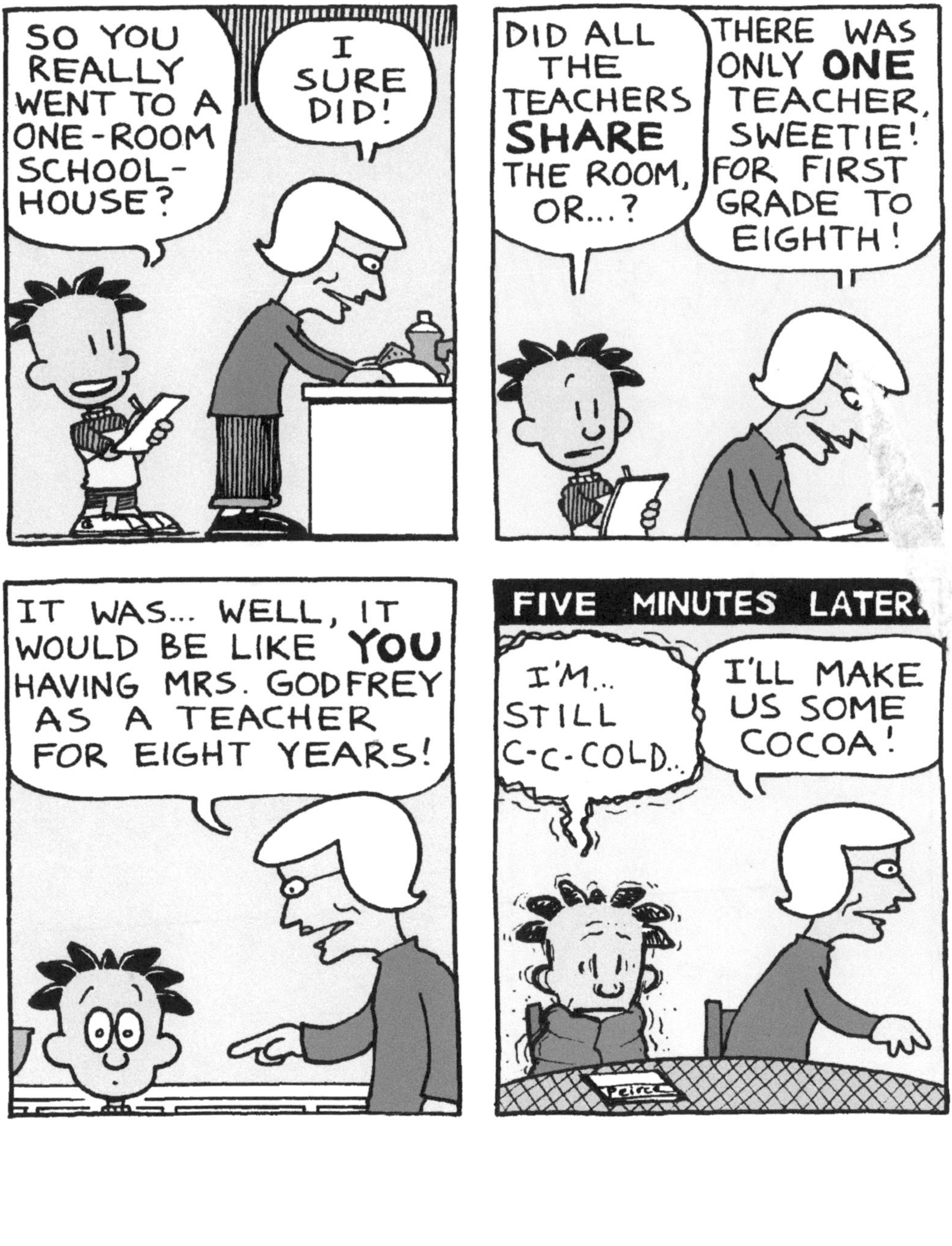
SO YOU REALLY WENT TO A ONE-ROOM SCHOOL-HOUSE?
I SURE DID!
DID ALL THE TEACHERS **SHARE** THE ROOM, OR...?
THERE WAS ONLY **ONE** TEACHER, SWEETIE! FOR FIRST GRADE TO EIGHTH!
IT WAS... WELL, IT WOULD BE LIKE **YOU** HAVING MRS. GODFREY AS A TEACHER FOR EIGHT YEARS!
FIVE MINUTES LATER...
I'M... STILL C-C-COLD...
I'LL MAKE US SOME COCOA!

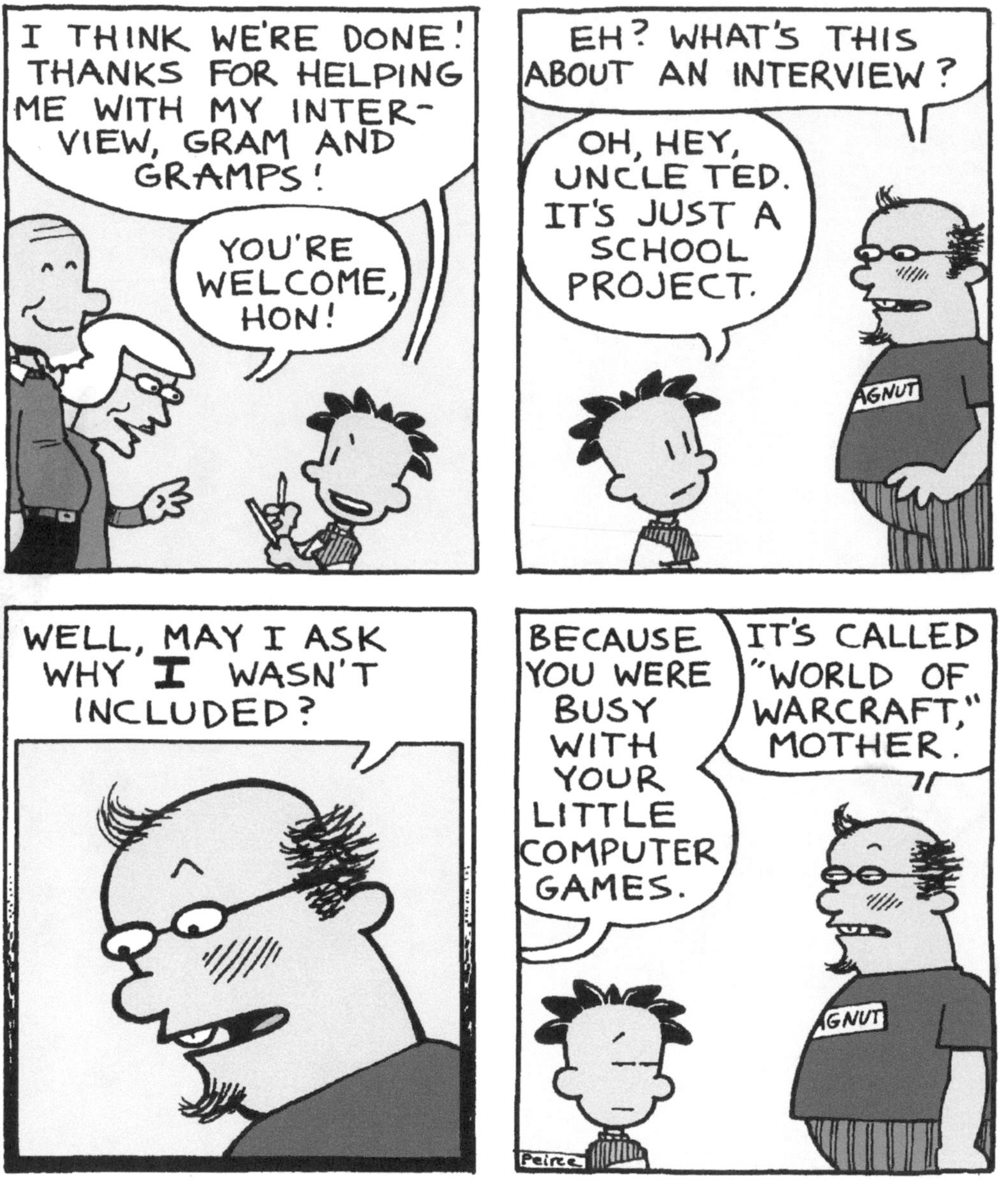
I THINK WE'RE DONE! THANKS FOR HELPING ME WITH MY INTER-VIEW, GRAM AND GRAMPS!
YOU'RE WELCOME, HON!
EH? WHAT'S THIS ABOUT AN INTERVIEW?
OH, HEY, UNCLE TED. IT'S JUST A SCHOOL PROJECT.
AGNUT
WELL, MAY I ASK WHY I WASN'T INCLUDED?
BECAUSE YOU WERE BUSY WITH YOUR LITTLE COMPUTER GAMES.
IT'S CALLED "WORLD OF WARCRAFT," MOTHER.
GNUT
Peirce

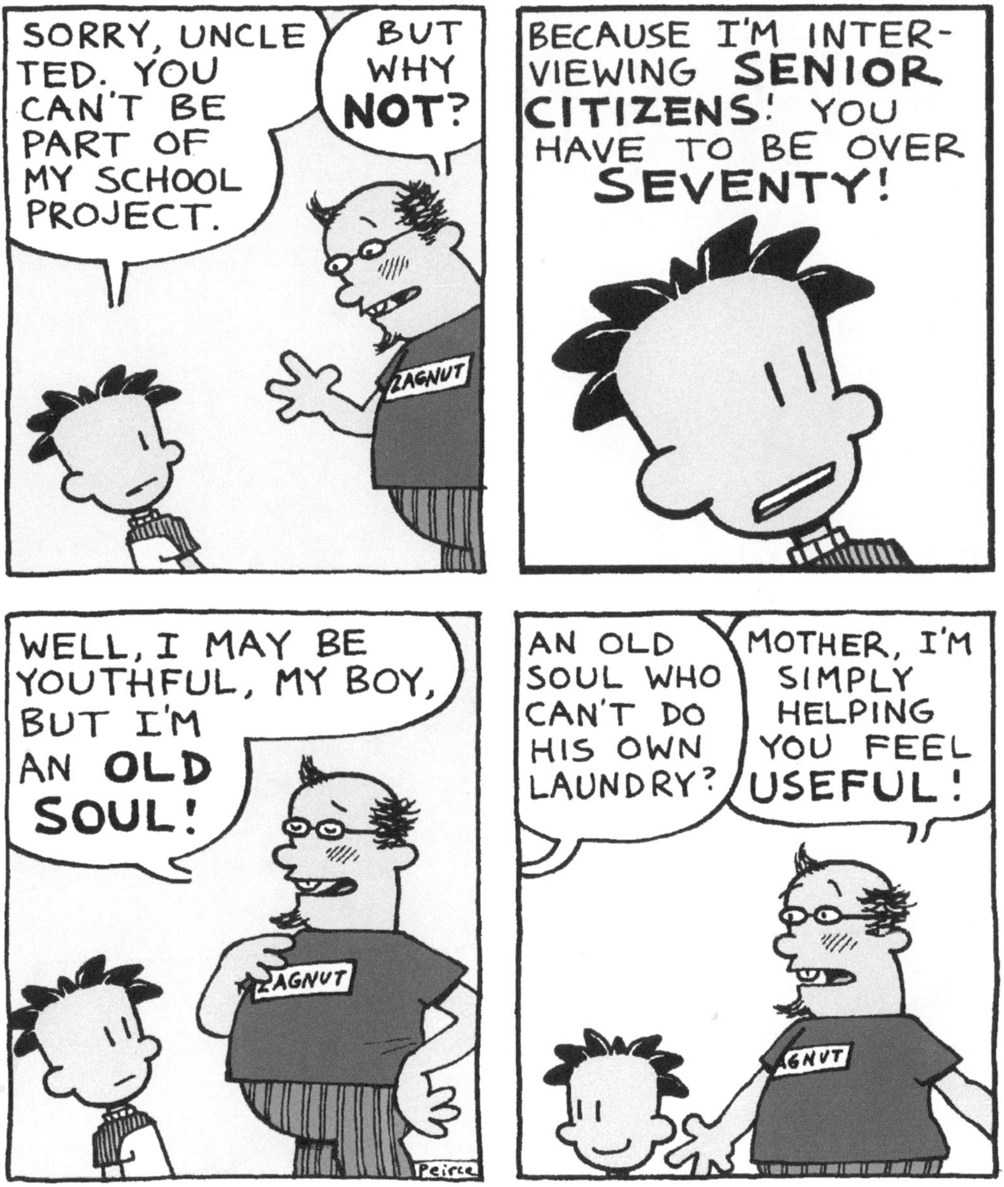
SORRY, UNCLE TED. YOU CAN'T BE PART OF MY SCHOOL PROJECT.
BUT WHY NOT?
BECAUSE I'M INTER-VIEWING SENIOR CITIZENS! YOU HAVE TO BE OVER SEVENTY!
WELL, I MAY BE YOUTHFUL, MY BOY, BUT I'M AN OLD SOUL!
AN OLD SOUL WHO CAN'T DO HIS OWN LAUNDRY?
MOTHER, I'M SIMPLY HELPING YOU FEEL USEFUL!
ZAGNUT
Peirce

HERE'S MY "SENIOR CITIZEN" REPORT, MS. CLARKE!

THANK YOU, NATE! WHO DID YOU INTERVIEW?

MY GRANDPARENTS! **BOTH** OF THEM! SO I INTERVIEWED **TWICE** AS MANY PEOPLE AS YOU ASKED US TO!

...AND IF THAT'S NOT ENOUGH TO GET ME EXTRA CREDIT, CHECK OUT WHAT'S ON THE LAST PAGE!

I INCLUDED GRAM'S RECIPE FOR MOLASSES CRINKLES.

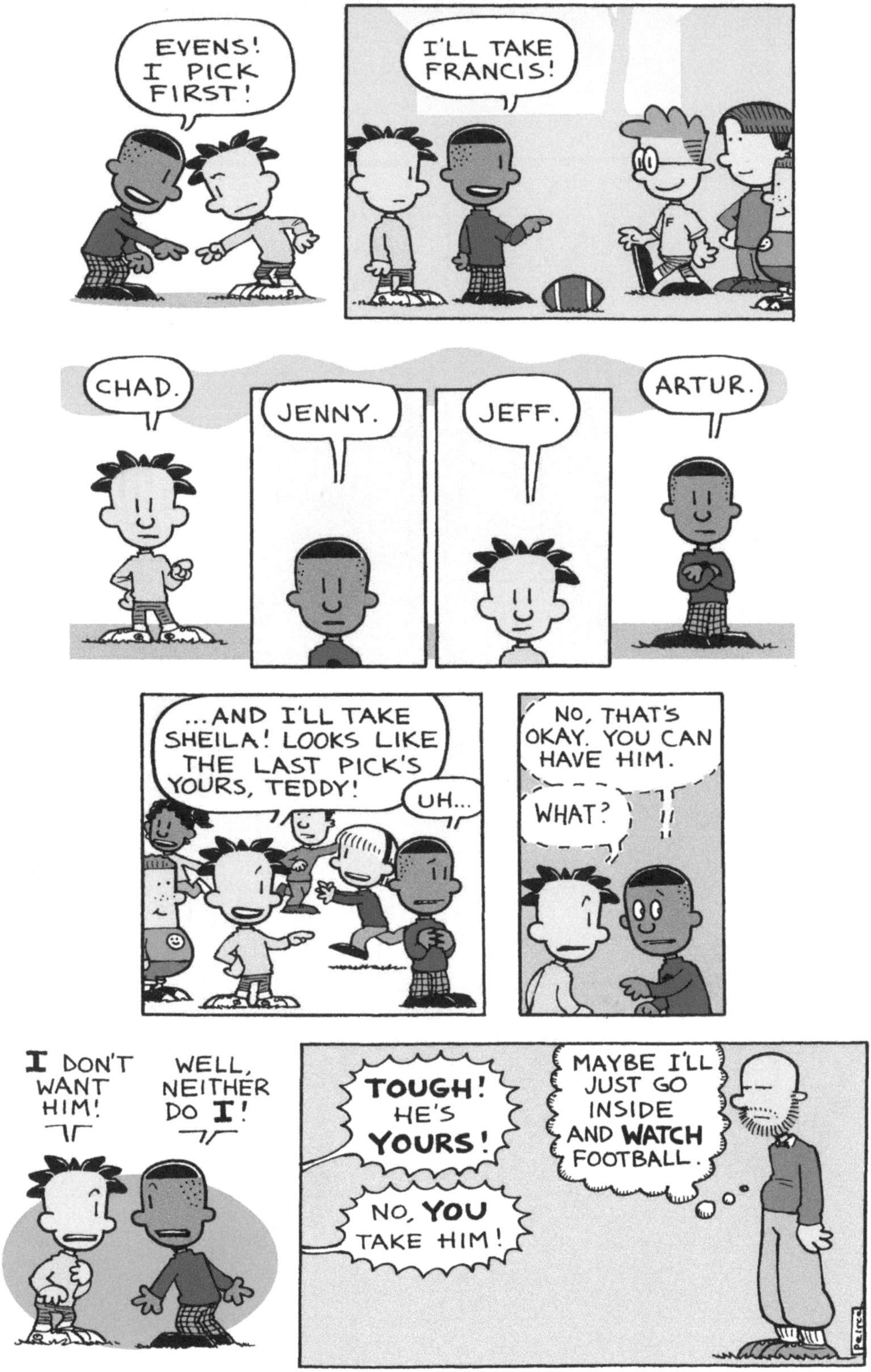
EVENS! I PICK FIRST!
I'LL TAKE FRANCIS!
CHAD.
JENNY.
JEFF.
ARTUR.
...AND I'LL TAKE SHEILA! LOOKS LIKE THE LAST PICK'S YOURS, TEDDY!
UH...
NO, THAT'S OKAY. YOU CAN HAVE HIM.
WHAT?
I DON'T WANT HIM!
WELL, NEITHER DO I!
TOUGH! HE'S YOURS!
NO, YOU TAKE HIM!
MAYBE I'LL JUST GO INSIDE AND WATCH FOOTBALL.

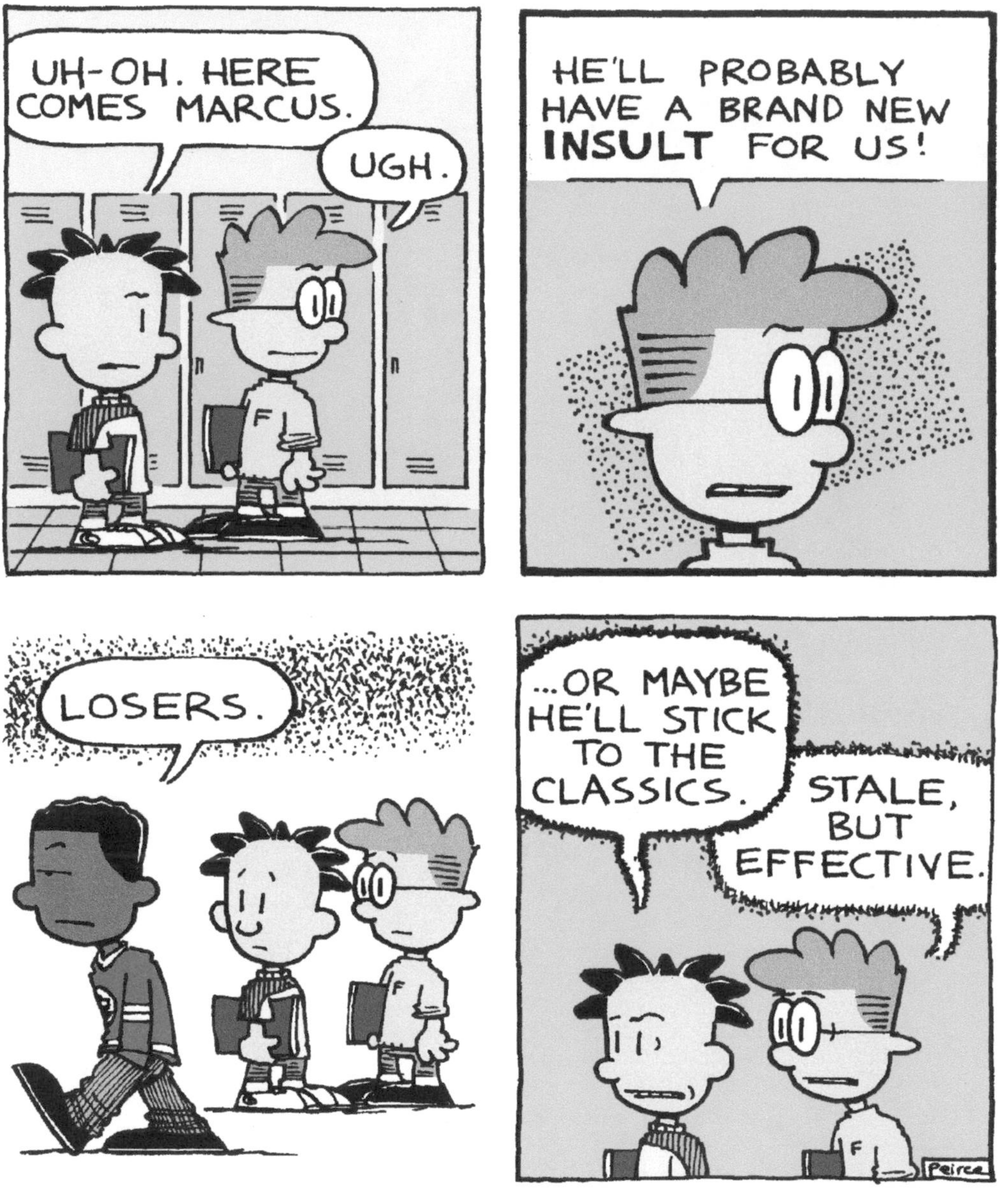
UH-OH. HERE COMES MARCUS.
UGH.
HE'LL PROBABLY HAVE A BRAND NEW **INSULT** FOR US!
LOSERS.
...OR MAYBE HE'LL STICK TO THE CLASSICS.
STALE, BUT EFFECTIVE.
Peirce

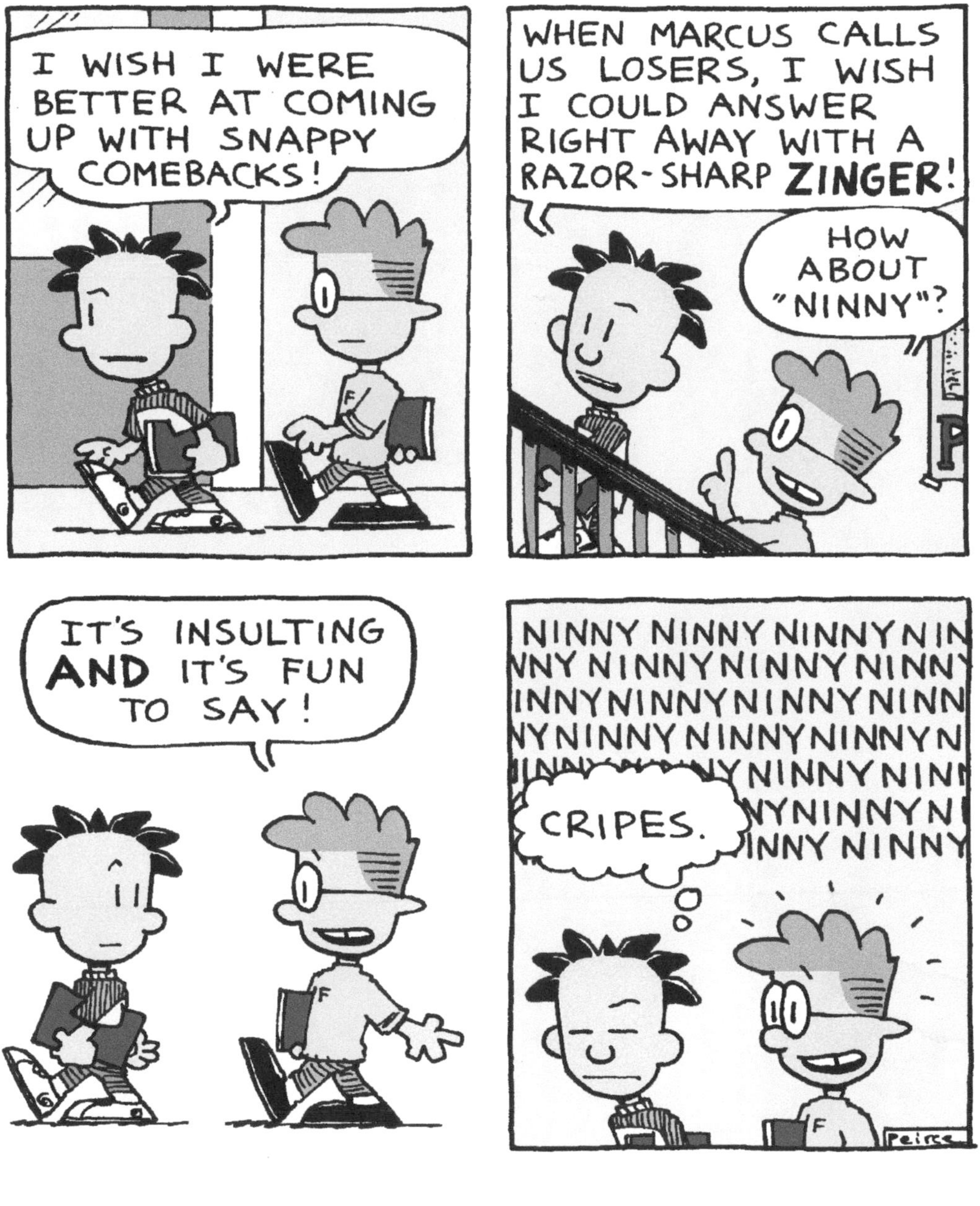
I WISH I WERE BETTER AT COMING UP WITH SNAPPY COMEBACKS!
WHEN MARCUS CALLS US LOSERS, I WISH I COULD ANSWER RIGHT AWAY WITH A RAZOR-SHARP **ZINGER**!
HOW ABOUT "NINNY"?
IT'S INSULTING **AND** IT'S FUN TO SAY!
NINNY NINNY NINNY NINNY
CRIPES.
Peirce

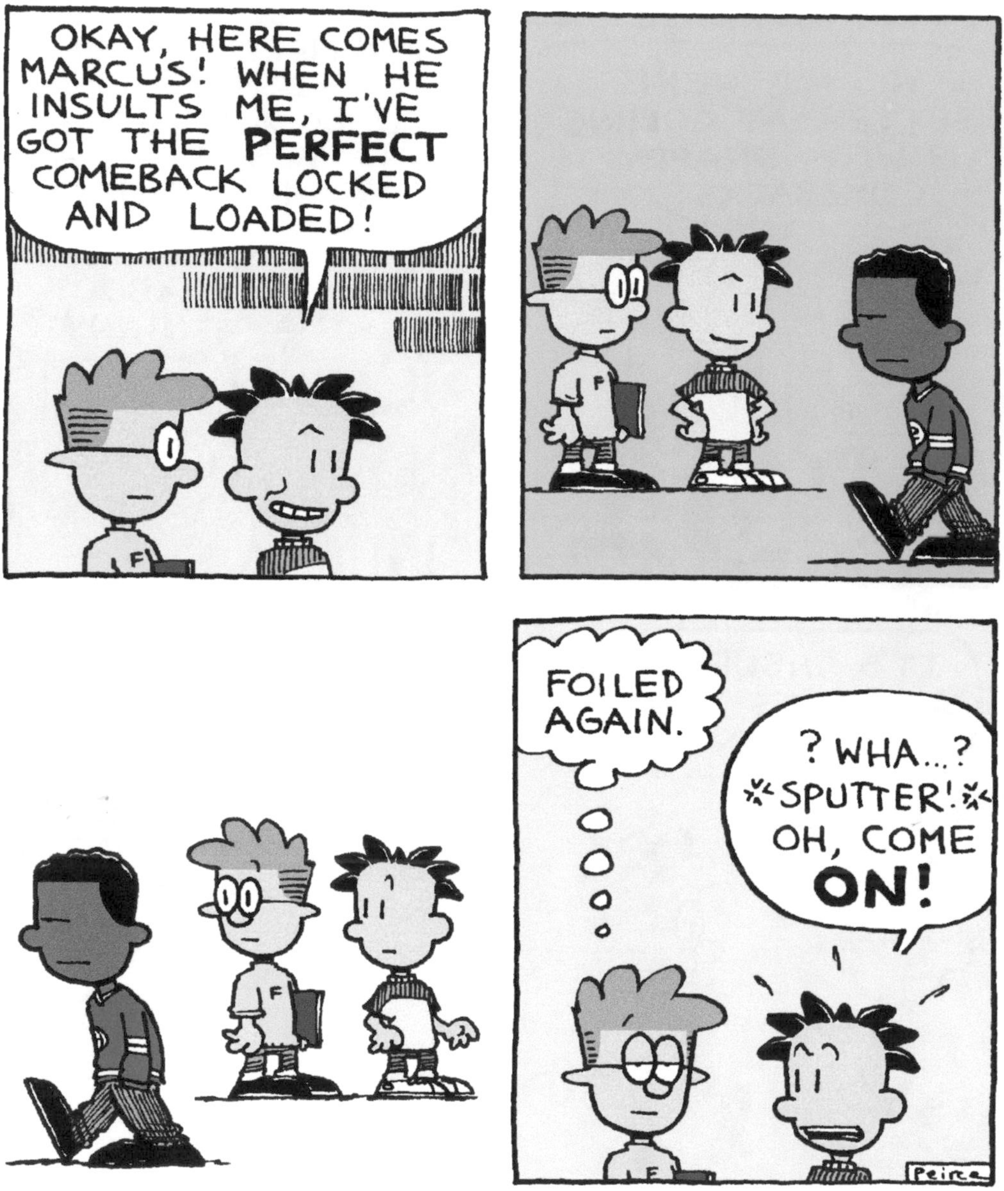
OKAY, HERE COMES MARCUS! WHEN HE INSULTS ME, I'VE GOT THE **PERFECT** COMEBACK LOCKED AND LOADED!
FOILED AGAIN.
? WHA...? SPUTTER! OH, COME **ON!**
Peirce

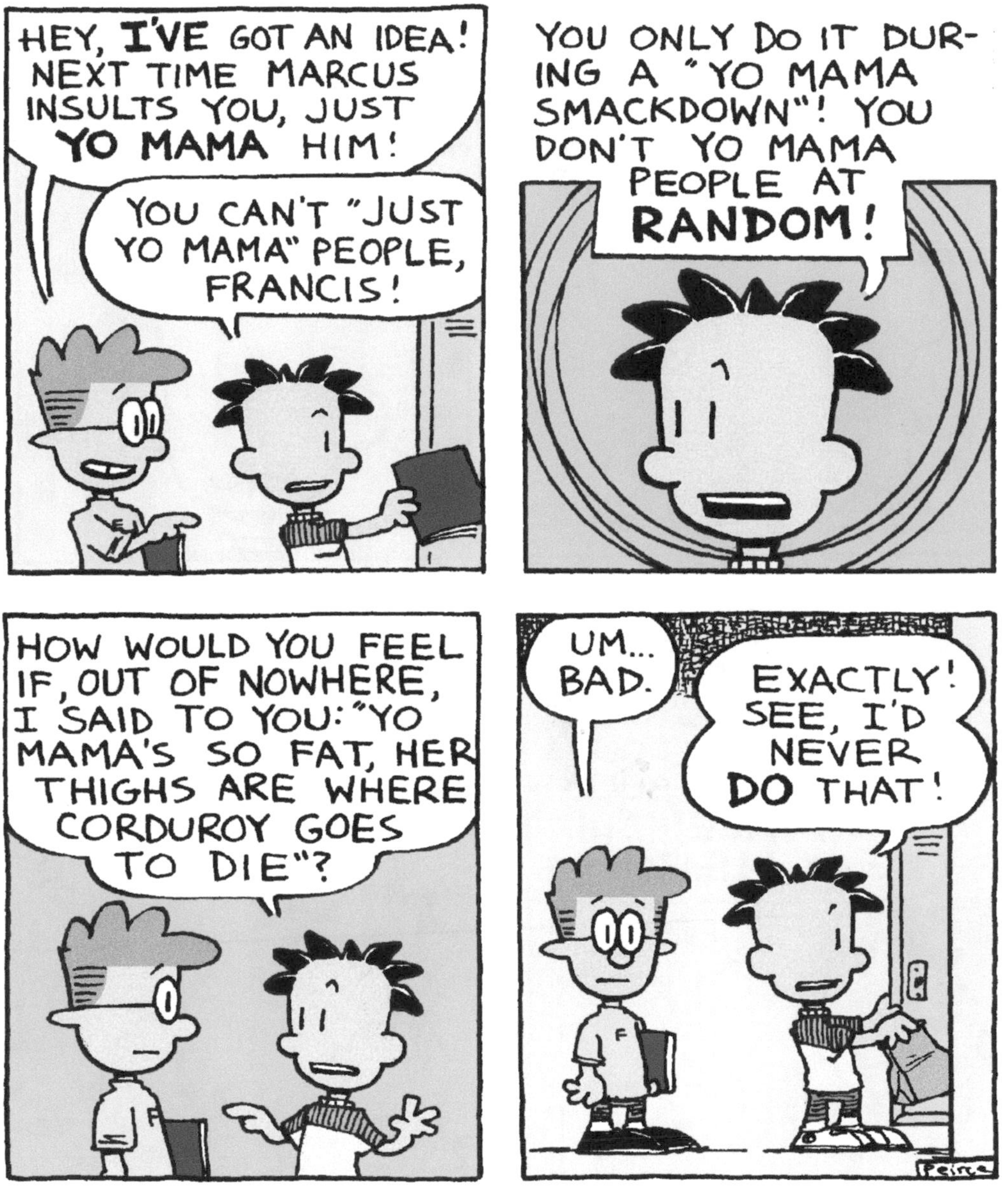
HEY, I'VE GOT AN IDEA! NEXT TIME MARCUS INSULTS YOU, JUST YO MAMA HIM!
YOU CAN'T "JUST YO MAMA" PEOPLE, FRANCIS!
YOU ONLY DO IT DURING A "YO MAMA SMACKDOWN"! YOU DON'T YO MAMA PEOPLE AT RANDOM!
HOW WOULD YOU FEEL IF, OUT OF NOWHERE, I SAID TO YOU: "YO MAMA'S SO FAT, HER THIGHS ARE WHERE CORDUROY GOES TO DIE"?
UM... BAD.
EXACTLY! SEE, I'D NEVER DO THAT!
Peirce

WHY DO YOU HAVE TO WAIT FOR MARCUS TO INSULT **YOU** BEFORE YOU INSULT **HIM**? WHY DON'T YOU GO **FIRST**?

FRANCIS, IF I JUST WALK UP TO MARCUS AND INSULT HIM, HE'LL **CLOCK** ME!

...BUT IF I COME UP WITH A WELL-TIMED, WITTY COMEBACK, **I'LL** BE THE GUY WHO PUT THE BULLY IN HIS **PLACE**! I'LL BE A **HERO**!

I'LL GET A STANDING OVATION... GIRLS WILL ADORE ME.... THE YEAR-BOOK WILL PR.... ...AGE A... MY IM... WAY

SOMEONE'S BEEN WATCHING TOO MANY TV MOVIES.

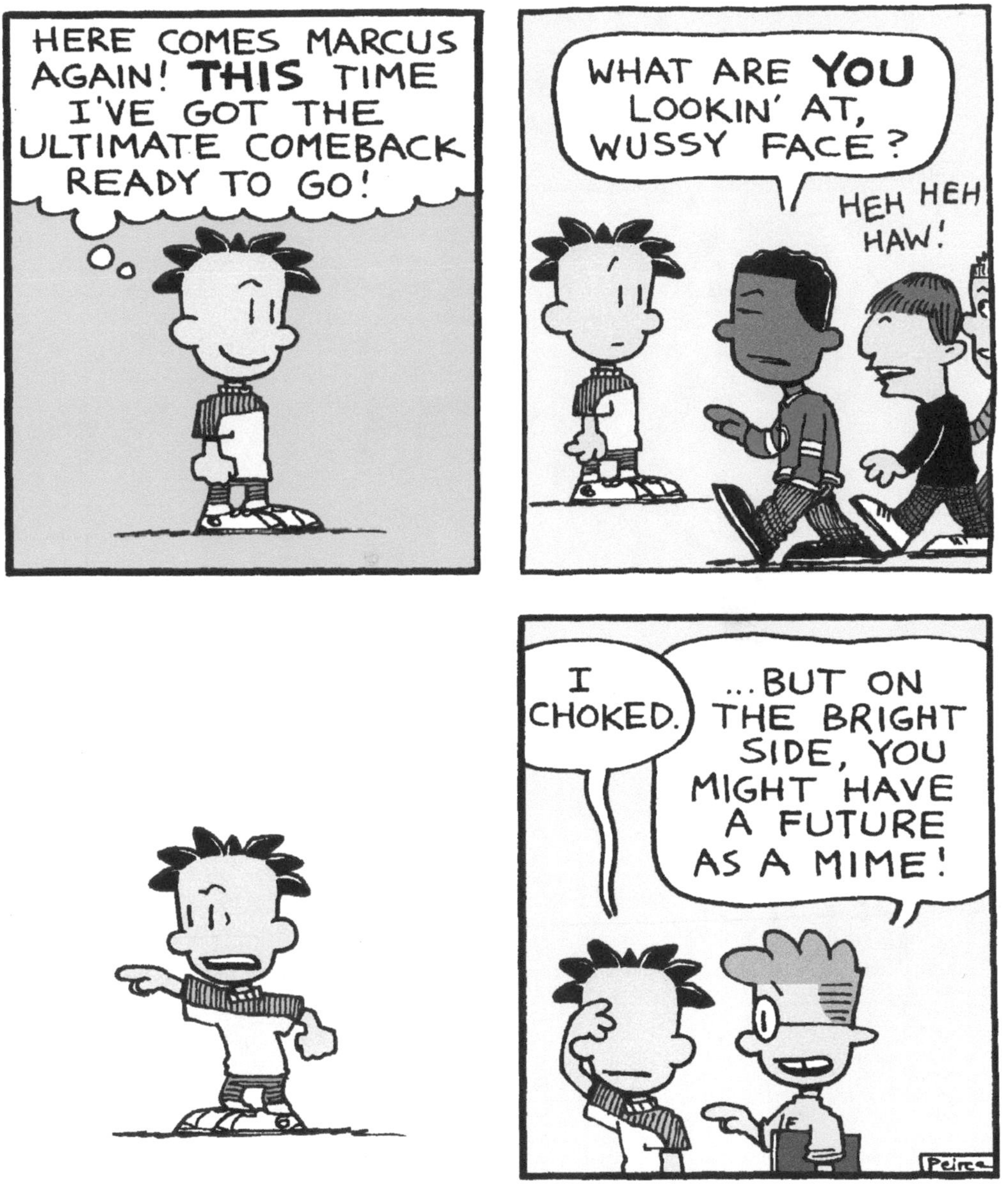
HERE COMES MARCUS AGAIN! **THIS** TIME I'VE GOT THE ULTIMATE COMEBACK READY TO GO!
WHAT ARE **YOU** LOOKIN' AT, WUSSY FACE?
HEH HEH HAW!
I CHOKED.
...BUT ON THE BRIGHT SIDE, YOU MIGHT HAVE A FUTURE AS A MIME!
Peirce

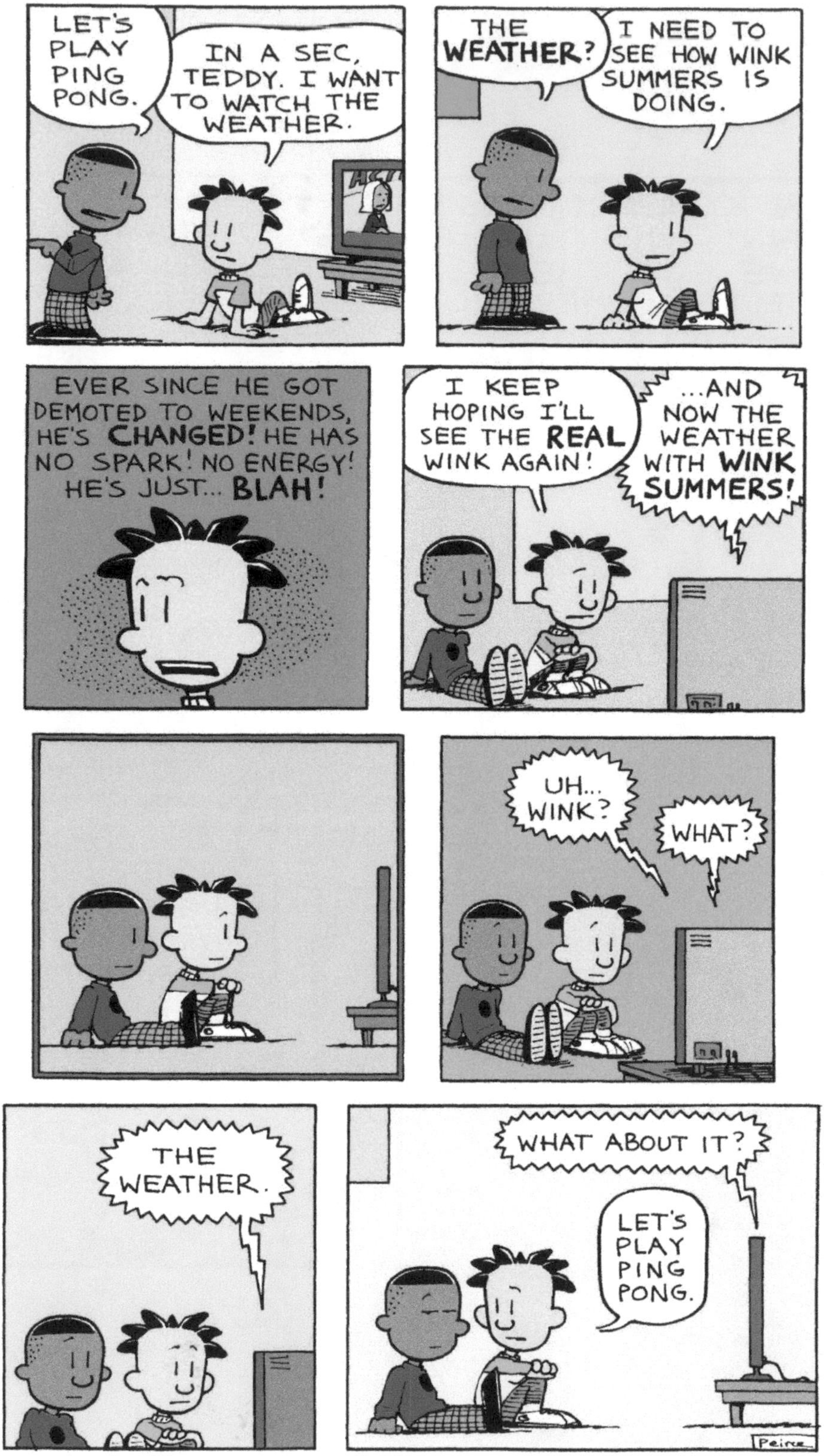
LET'S PLAY PING PONG.
IN A SEC, TEDDY. I WANT TO WATCH THE WEATHER.
THE WEATHER?
I NEED TO SEE HOW WINK SUMMERS IS DOING.
EVER SINCE HE GOT DEMOTED TO WEEKENDS, HE'S CHANGED! HE HAS NO SPARK! NO ENERGY! HE'S JUST... BLAH!
I KEEP HOPING I'LL SEE THE REAL WINK AGAIN!
...AND NOW THE WEATHER WITH WINK SUMMERS!
UH... WINK?
WHAT?
THE WEATHER.
WHAT ABOUT IT?
LET'S PLAY PING PONG.
Peirce

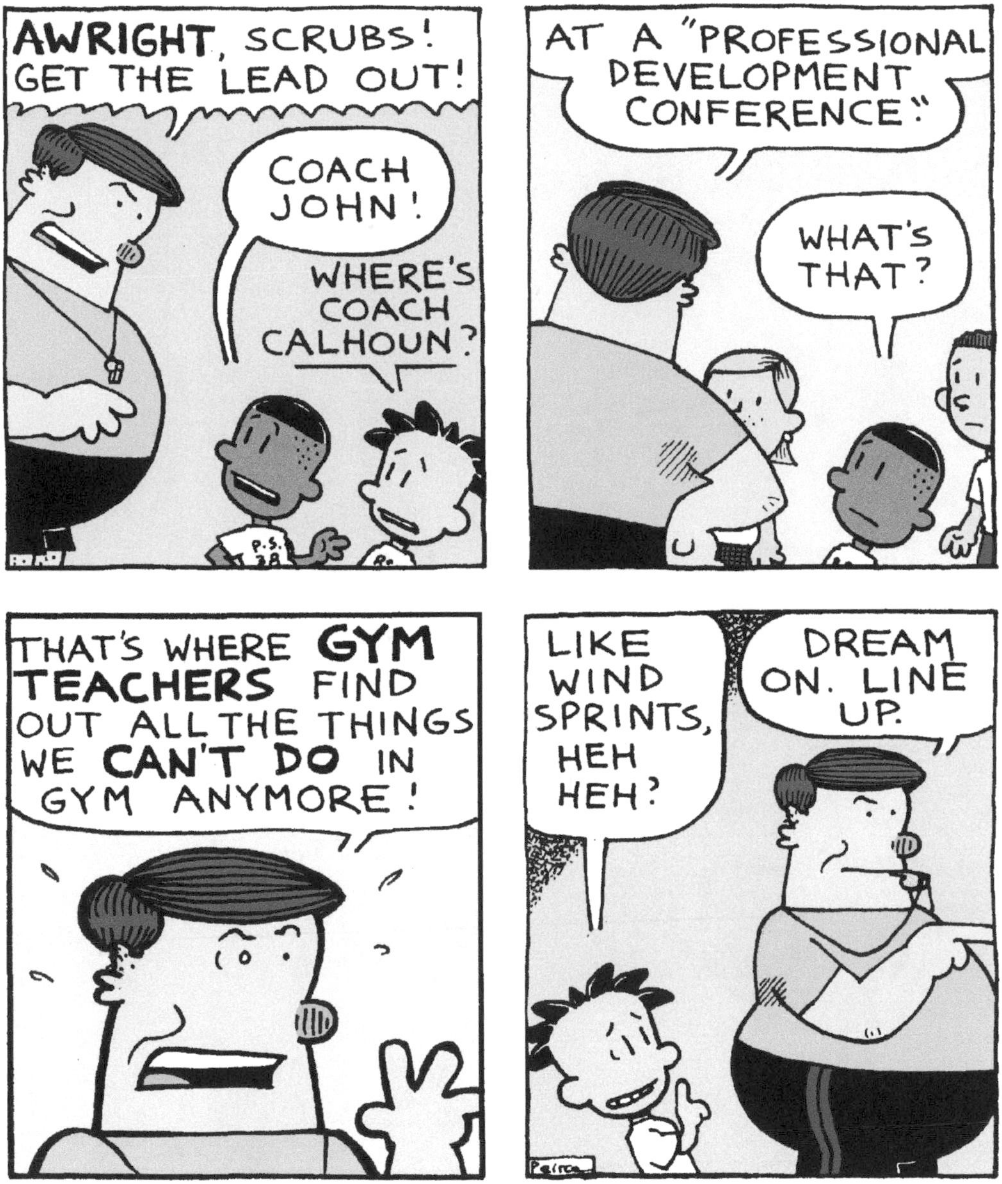
AWRIGHT, SCRUBS! GET THE LEAD OUT!
COACH JOHN!
WHERE'S COACH CALHOUN?
P.S. 38
AT A "PROFESSIONAL DEVELOPMENT CONFERENCE."
WHAT'S THAT?
THAT'S WHERE GYM TEACHERS FIND OUT ALL THE THINGS WE CAN'T DO IN GYM ANYMORE!
LIKE WIND SPRINTS, HEH HEH?
DREAM ON. LINE UP.
Peirce

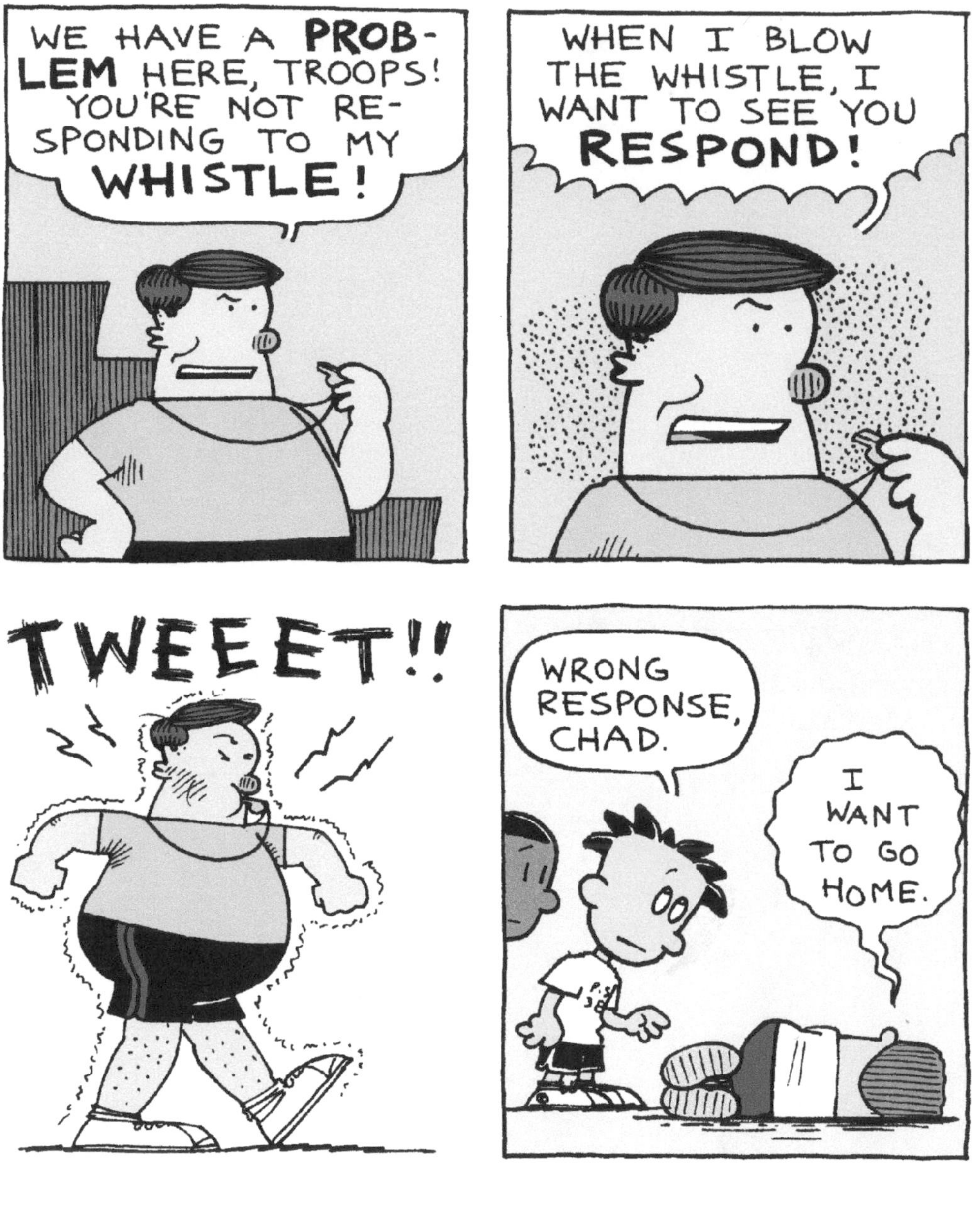
WE HAVE A PROBLEM HERE, TROOPS! YOU'RE NOT RESPONDING TO MY WHISTLE!
WHEN I BLOW THE WHISTLE, I WANT TO SEE YOU RESPOND!
TWEEET!!
WRONG RESPONSE, CHAD.
I WANT TO GO HOME.

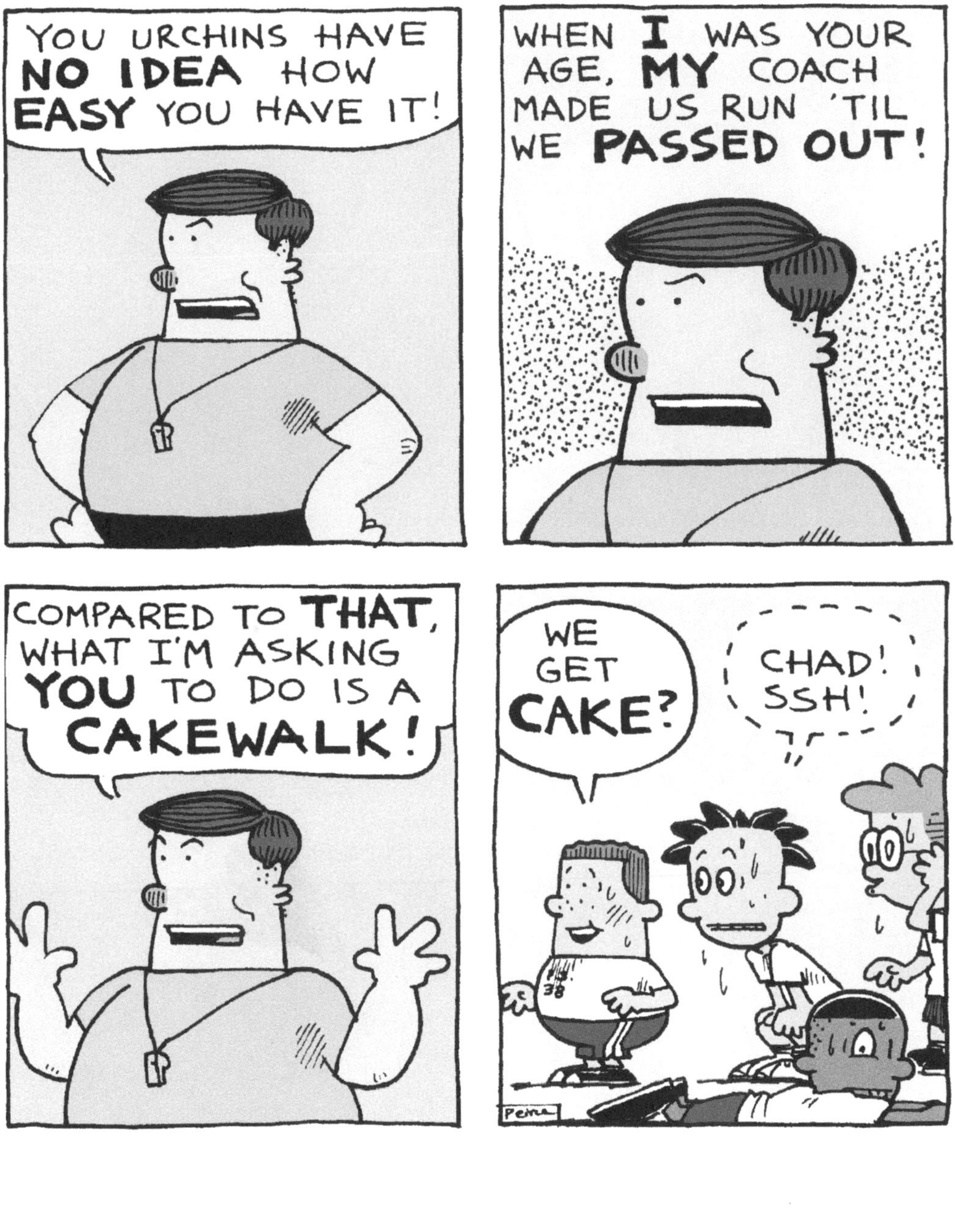
YOU URCHINS HAVE **NO IDEA** HOW **EASY** YOU HAVE IT!
WHEN **I** WAS YOUR AGE, **MY** COACH MADE US RUN 'TIL WE **PASSED OUT**!
COMPARED TO **THAT**, WHAT I'M ASKING **YOU** TO DO IS A **CAKEWALK**!
WE GET **CAKE**?
CHAD! SSH!
38
Peirce

WOW, COACH! ARE WE EVER GLAD TO SEE YOU!
WELL, THANKS, BOYS!
WATER BREAK??
YOU DON'T NEED NO STINKIN' WATER BREAK!
DID WE MENTION HOW GLAD WE ARE TO SEE YOU?
WE'RE ECSTATIC.
Peirce

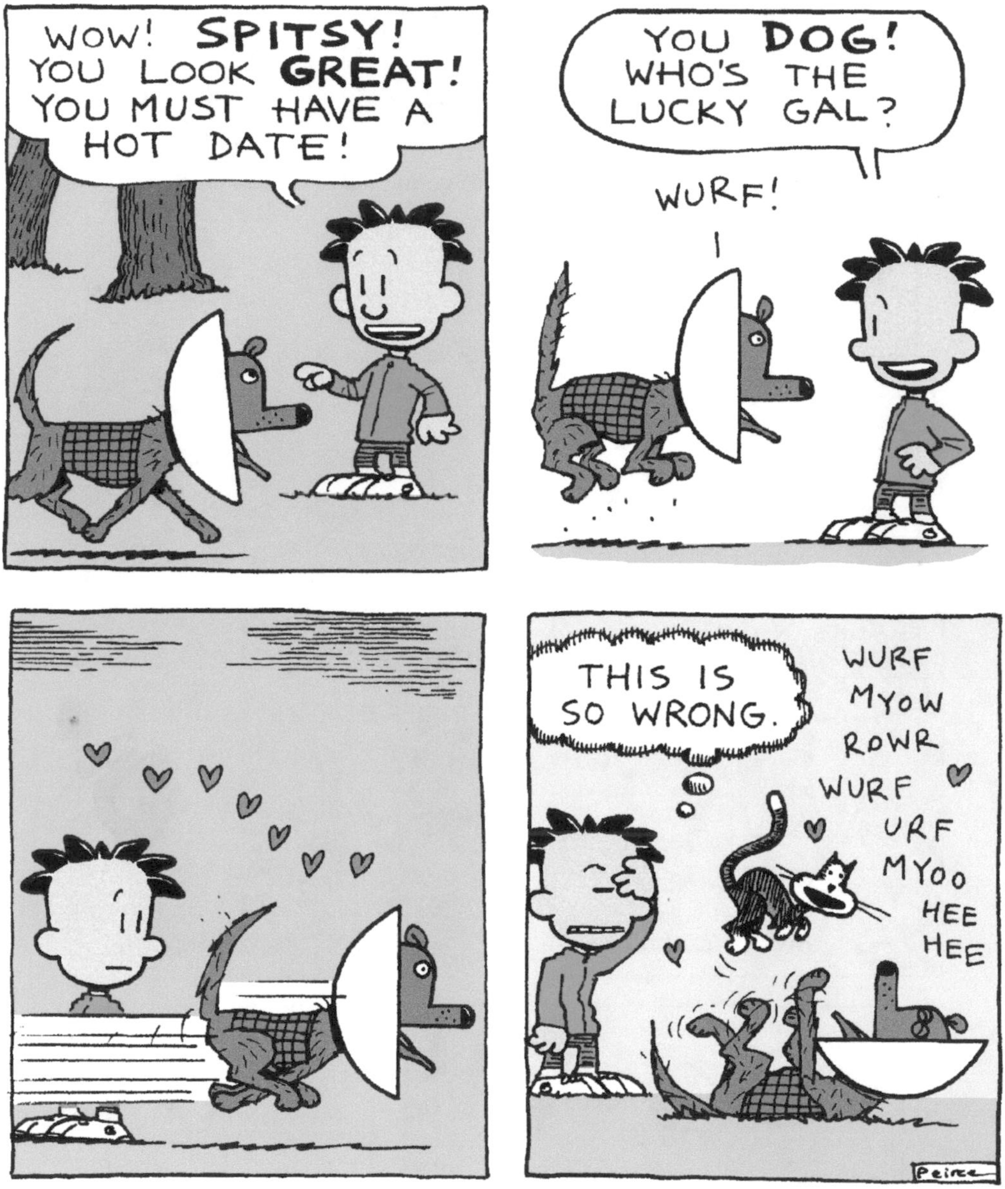
WOW! SPITSY! YOU LOOK GREAT! YOU MUST HAVE A HOT DATE!
YOU DOG! WHO'S THE LUCKY GAL?
WURF!
THIS IS SO WRONG.
WURF
MYOW
ROWR
WURF
URF
MYOO
HEE
HEE
Peirce

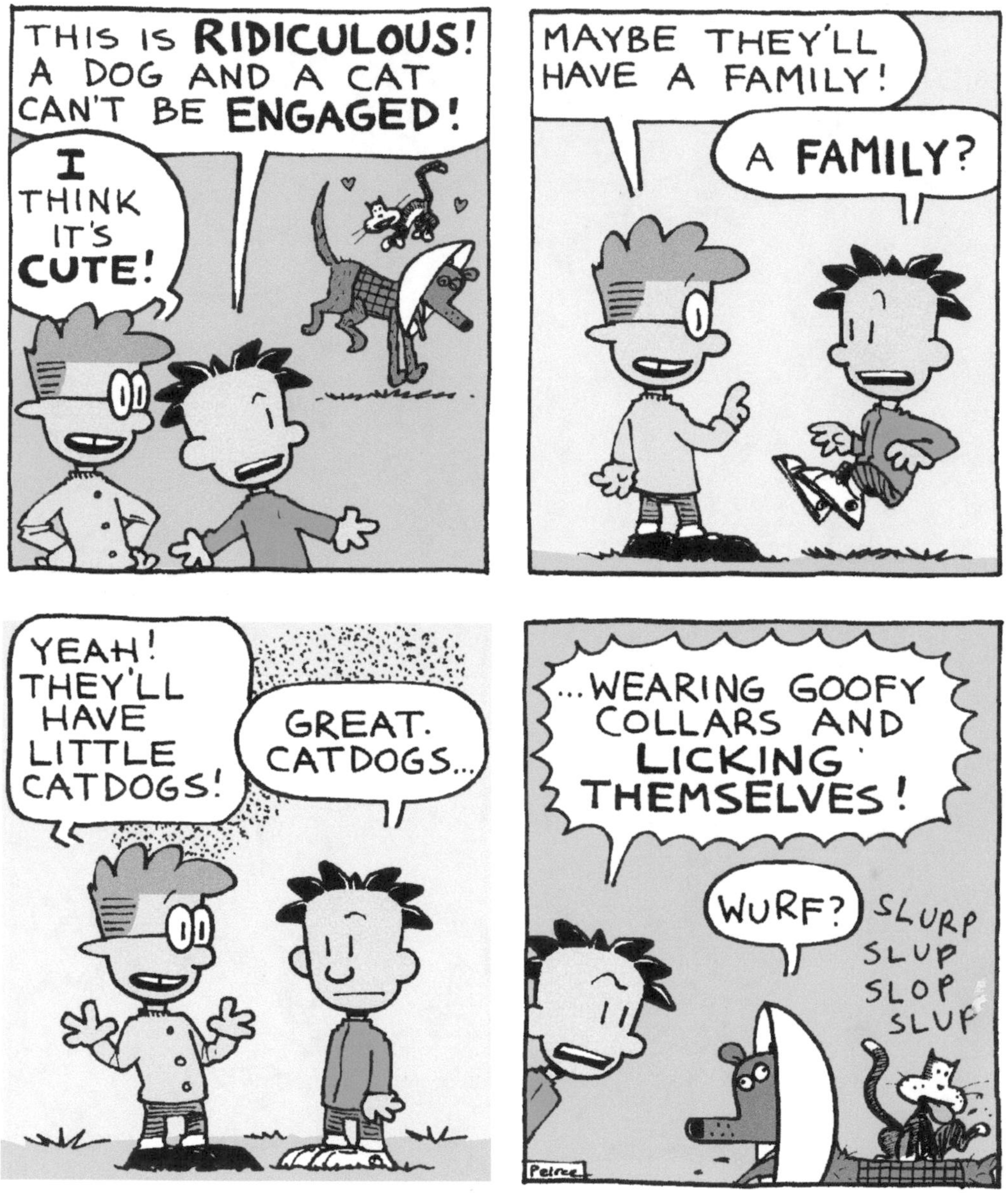
THIS IS RIDICULOUS! A DOG AND A CAT CAN'T BE ENGAGED!
I THINK IT'S CUTE!
MAYBE THEY'LL HAVE A FAMILY!
A FAMILY?
YEAH! THEY'LL HAVE LITTLE CATDOGS!
GREAT. CATDOGS...
...WEARING GOOFY COLLARS AND LICKING THEMSELVES!
WURF?
SLURP
SLUP
SLOP
SLUF
Peirce

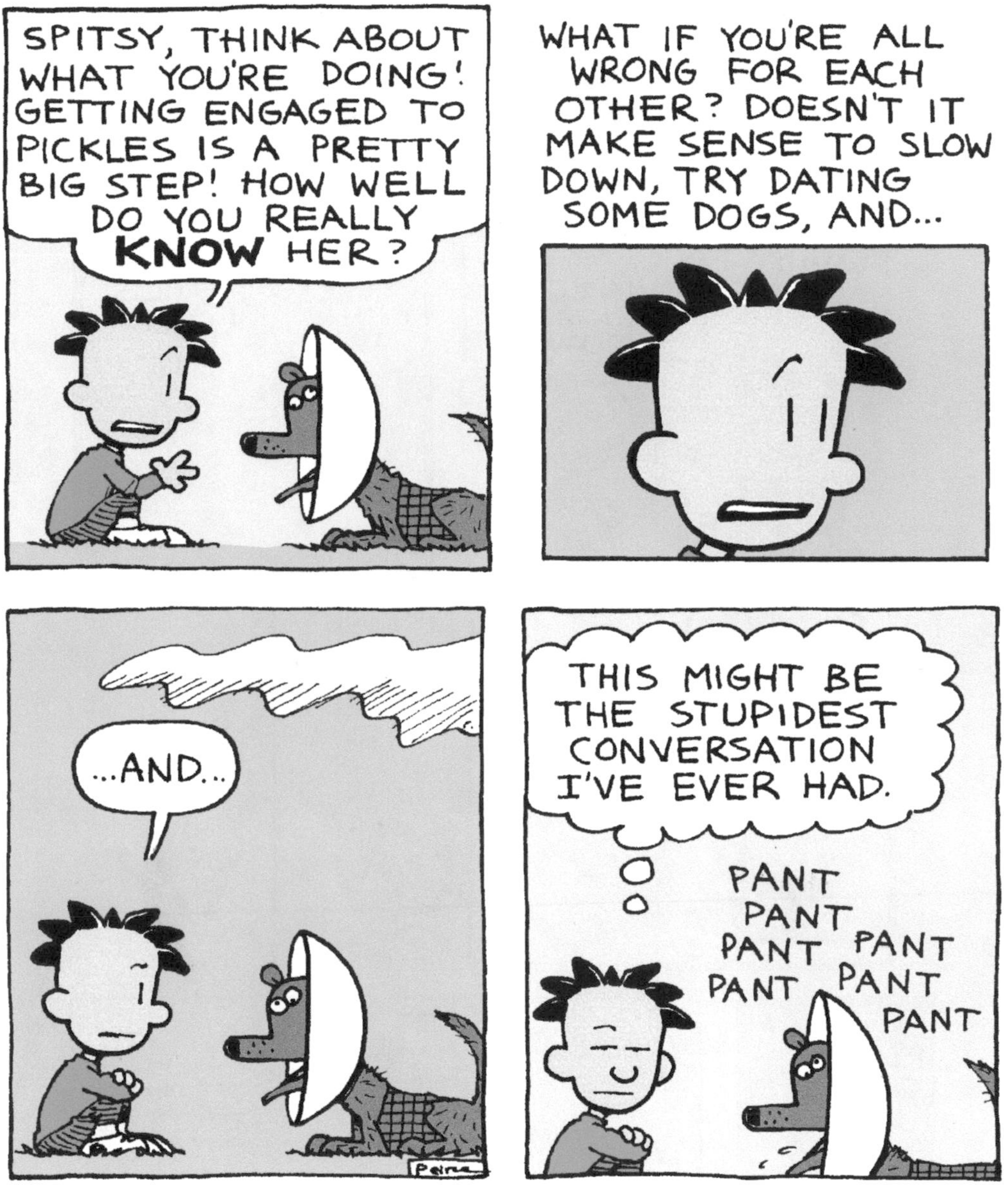
SPITSY, THINK ABOUT WHAT YOU'RE DOING! GETTING ENGAGED TO PICKLES IS A PRETTY BIG STEP! HOW WELL DO YOU REALLY **KNOW** HER?
WHAT IF YOU'RE ALL WRONG FOR EACH OTHER? DOESN'T IT MAKE SENSE TO SLOW DOWN, TRY DATING SOME DOGS, AND...
...AND...
THIS MIGHT BE THE STUPIDEST CONVERSATION I'VE EVER HAD.
PANT PANT PANT PANT PANT PANT PANT

HAVING TROUBLE FINDING SOMETHING?

UH, NO, THAT'S OKAY.

OH, LET ME HELP YOU! WE'RE REORGANIZING THE STORE, AND EVERYTHING'S ALL WILLY-NILLY!

IT'S...UM... ✳KOFF!✳ IT'S CALLED "BETHANY."

AH, THE **COMIC STRIP!** WE **USED** TO SHELVE THOSE TREASURIES IN THE "HUMOR" SECTION, BUT NO MORE!

Peirce

TO THE TEEN ROMANCE AISLE!

CRIPES.

EW!

YOUNG MAN, WE DON'T **THROW** THINGS HERE AT THE BOOK LOFT!

S-SORRY. IT... UH... SLIPPED OUT OF MY HAND.

WELL, WHEN IT "SLIPPED," THE **COVER** WAS TORN! YOU'LL HAVE TO BUY THIS!

'KAY.

☀SNICKER!☀... YOU'RE BUYING A "**BETHANY**" TREASURY?

IT'S FOR MY **SISTER**!

THEN WHY WERE **YOU** SITTING ON THE FLOOR **READING** IT WHEN I FOUND YOU?

I HATE MYSELF.

KA-CHING!

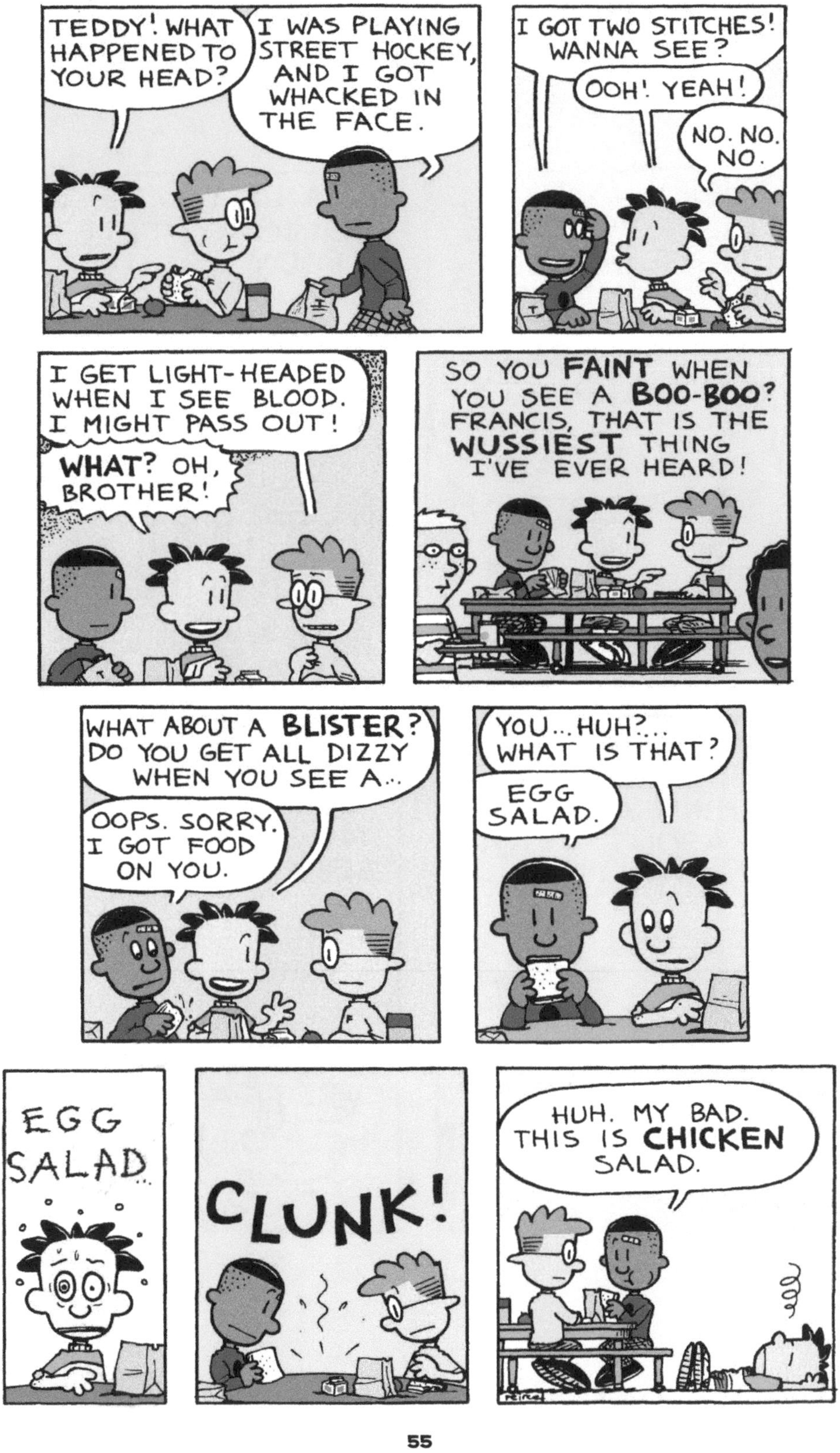
TEDDY! WHAT HAPPENED TO YOUR HEAD?
I WAS PLAYING STREET HOCKEY, AND I GOT WHACKED IN THE FACE.
I GOT TWO STITCHES! WANNA SEE?
OOH! YEAH!
NO. NO. NO.
I GET LIGHT-HEADED WHEN I SEE BLOOD. I MIGHT PASS OUT!
WHAT? OH, BROTHER!
SO YOU FAINT WHEN YOU SEE A BOO-BOO? FRANCIS, THAT IS THE WUSSIEST THING I'VE EVER HEARD!
WHAT ABOUT A BLISTER? DO YOU GET ALL DIZZY WHEN YOU SEE A...
OOPS. SORRY. I GOT FOOD ON YOU.
YOU... HUH?... WHAT IS THAT?
EGG SALAD.
EGG SALAD...
CLUNK!
HUH. MY BAD. THIS IS CHICKEN SALAD.

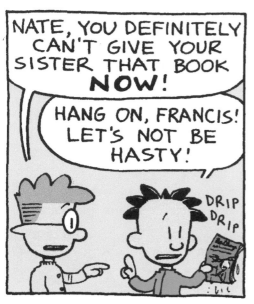

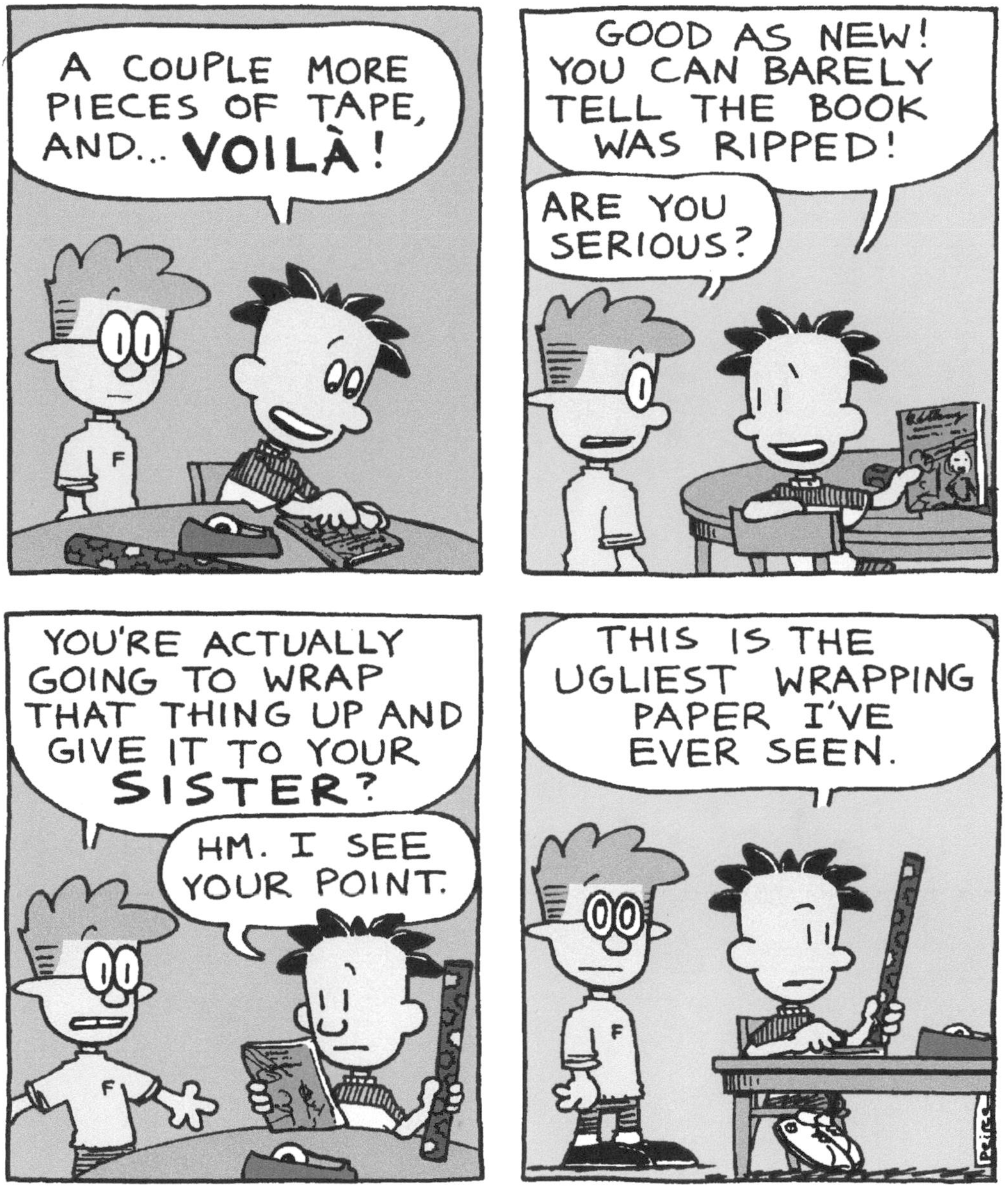
A COUPLE MORE PIECES OF TAPE, AND... VOILÀ!
GOOD AS NEW! YOU CAN BARELY TELL THE BOOK WAS RIPPED!
ARE YOU SERIOUS?
YOU'RE ACTUALLY GOING TO WRAP THAT THING UP AND GIVE IT TO YOUR SISTER?
HM. I SEE YOUR POINT.
THIS IS THE UGLIEST WRAPPING PAPER I'VE EVER SEEN.
PEIRCE

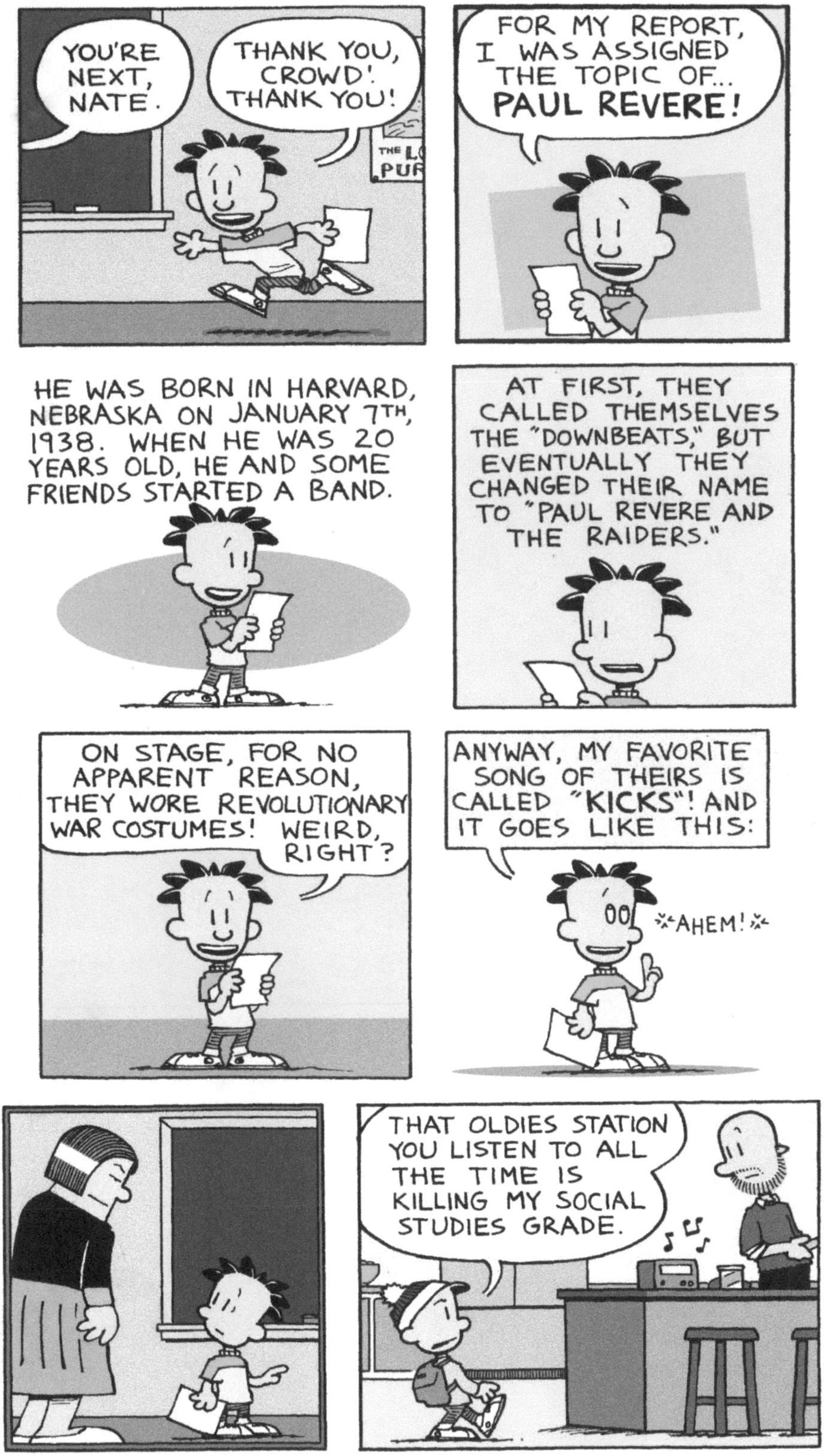

YOU'RE NEXT, NATE.
THANK YOU, CROWD! THANK YOU!
FOR MY REPORT, I WAS ASSIGNED THE TOPIC OF... PAUL REVERE!
HE WAS BORN IN HARVARD, NEBRASKA ON JANUARY 7TH, 1938. WHEN HE WAS 20 YEARS OLD, HE AND SOME FRIENDS STARTED A BAND.
AT FIRST, THEY CALLED THEMSELVES THE "DOWNBEATS," BUT EVENTUALLY THEY CHANGED THEIR NAME TO "PAUL REVERE AND THE RAIDERS."
ON STAGE, FOR NO APPARENT REASON, THEY WORE REVOLUTIONARY WAR COSTUMES! WEIRD, RIGHT?
ANYWAY, MY FAVORITE SONG OF THEIRS IS CALLED "KICKS"! AND IT GOES LIKE THIS:
AHEM!
THAT OLDIES STATION YOU LISTEN TO ALL THE TIME IS KILLING MY SOCIAL STUDIES GRADE.

I'M NOT VERY GOOD AT DRAWING.

DAD, **RELAX**! IT'S JUST A **GAME**!

THE SCRIBBLE GAME ISN'T ABOUT MAKING PERFECT DRAWINGS! IT'S ABOUT HAVING **FUN**! YOU **CAN'T** DO IT **WRONG**!

YES, YOU CAN.

IT'S A DUCK.

Peirce

NO OFFENSE, DAD, BUT TO PLAY THE SCRIBBLE GAME, YOU NEED A LITTLE IMAGINATION!

YOU WERE SUPPOSED TO TURN THE SCRIBBLE **INTO** SOMETHING!

I **DID!**

I TURNED IT INTO A FIGURE EIGHT!

IT ALREADY **WAS** A FIGURE EIGHT.

NO, IT WAS A SIX. SEE, I CLOSED THE LOOP.

SO YOU WANT ME TO MAKE A NEW YEAR'S RESOLUTION, FRANCIS? OKAY, FINE!

I RESOLVE NOT TO GET ANY DETENTIONS FOR A WHOLE YEAR!

MMPH!

HEH HEH!

WA HA HA HA HA HA HA

WHAT WE HAVE HERE IS A COMPLETE LACK OF RESPECT.

THE WEEK'S HALF OVER, GINA, AND NATE HASN'T GOT A SINGLE DETENTION!

THERE'S STILL PLENTY OF TIME.

YEAH, BUT HE'S GOT ALL THE TEACHERS EATING OUT OF THE PALM OF HIS HAND!

OH, **PLEASE**! THE TEACHERS **HATE** HIM!

DON'T BE LITTERB[U]

KEEP OUR CL[E]AN

THE IDEA THAT HE COULD SUDDENLY BECOME THEIR **FAVORITE** IS A TOTAL **JOKE**!

...AND THEN THE CAMEL SAYS: "DUCK? **WHAT** DUCK?"

HA HA HA HA! VERY FUNNY, SIR!

!!

Pierce

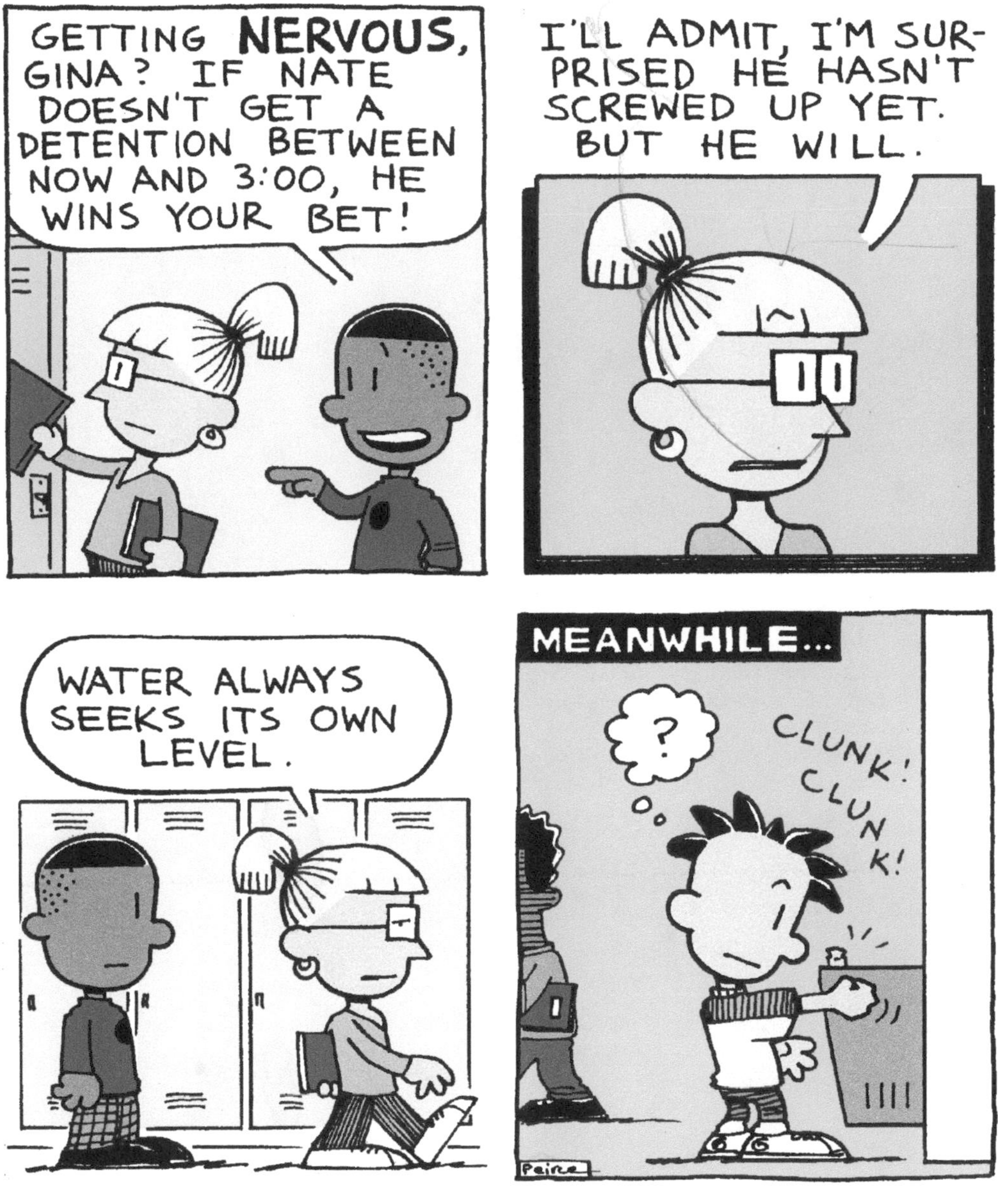
GETTING NERVOUS, GINA? IF NATE DOESN'T GET A DETENTION BETWEEN NOW AND 3:00, HE WINS YOUR BET!
I'LL ADMIT, I'M SURPRISED HE HASN'T SCREWED UP YET. BUT HE WILL.
WATER ALWAYS SEEKS ITS OWN LEVEL.
MEANWHILE...
?
CLUNK! CLUNK!
Peirce

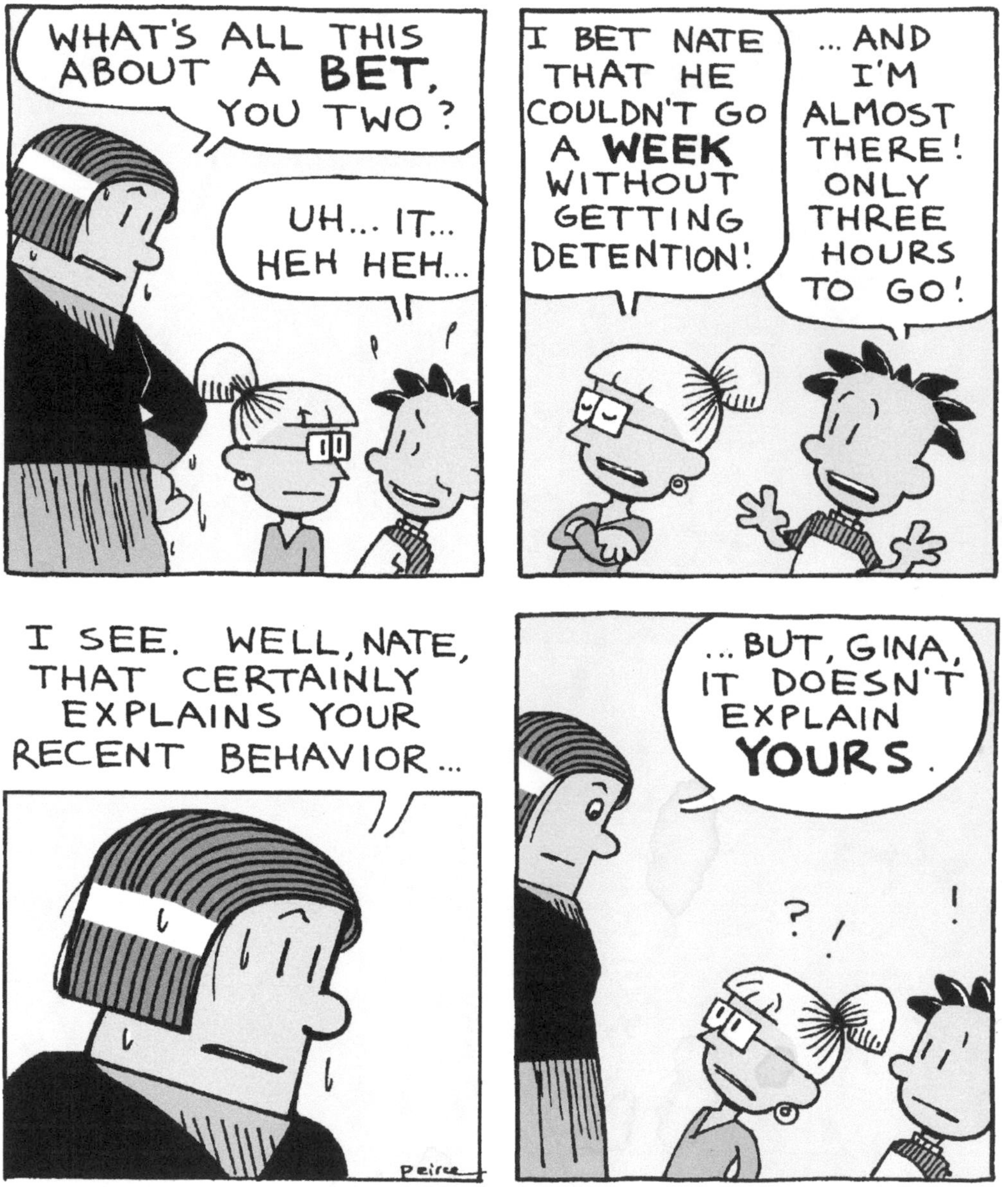
WHAT'S ALL THIS ABOUT A **BET**, YOU TWO?
UH... IT... HEH HEH...
I BET NATE THAT HE COULDN'T GO A **WEEK** WITHOUT GETTING DETENTION!
... AND I'M ALMOST THERE! ONLY THREE HOURS TO GO!
I SEE. WELL, NATE, THAT CERTAINLY EXPLAINS YOUR RECENT BEHAVIOR...
peirce
... BUT, GINA, IT DOESN'T EXPLAIN **YOURS**.
? !
!

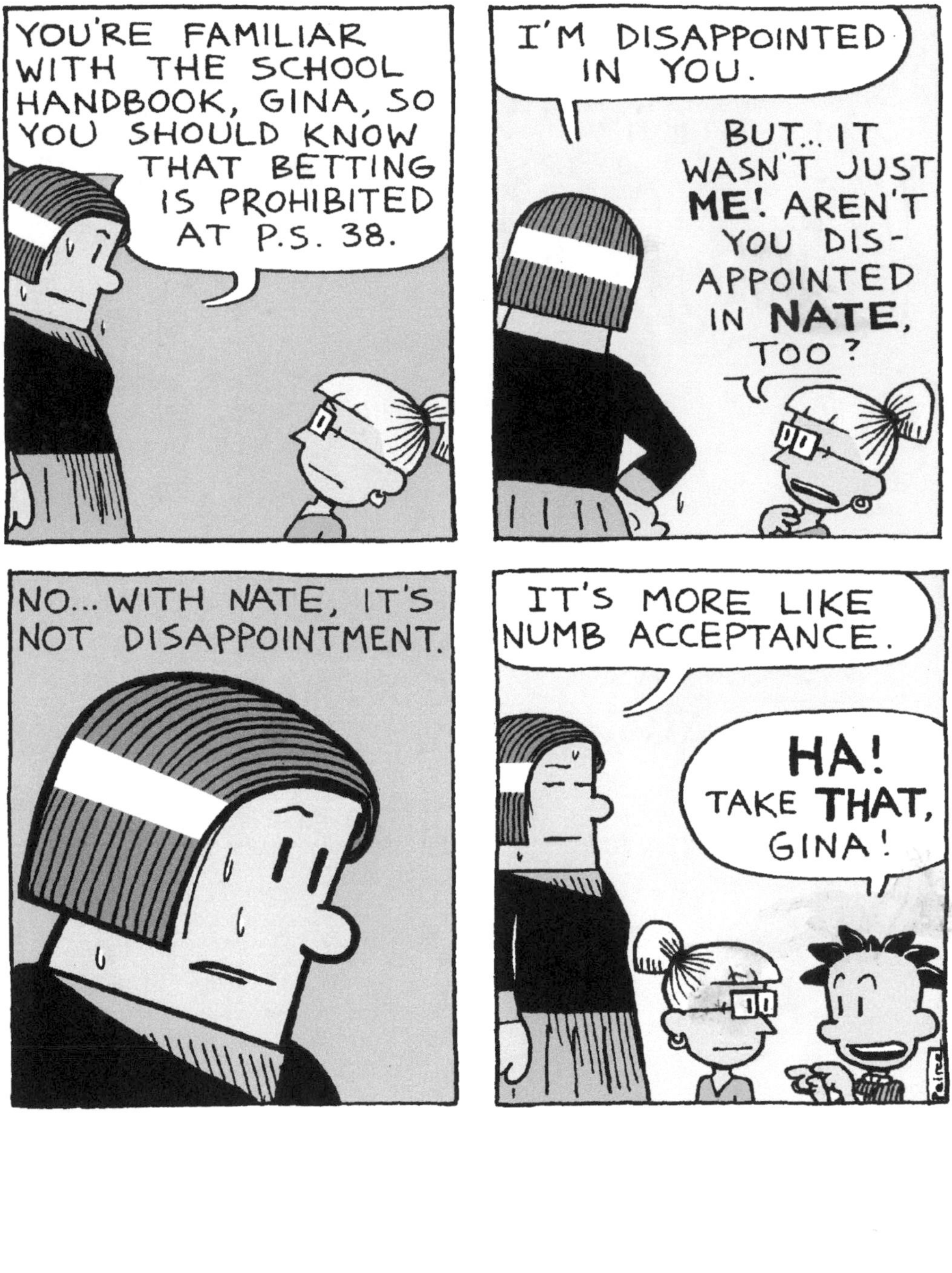
YOU'RE FAMILIAR WITH THE SCHOOL HANDBOOK, GINA, SO YOU SHOULD KNOW THAT BETTING IS PROHIBITED AT P.S. 38.
I'M DISAPPOINTED IN YOU.
BUT... IT WASN'T JUST **ME**! AREN'T YOU DIS-APPOINTED IN **NATE**, TOO?
NO... WITH NATE, IT'S NOT DISAPPOINTMENT.
IT'S MORE LIKE NUMB ACCEPTANCE.
HA! TAKE **THAT**, GINA!

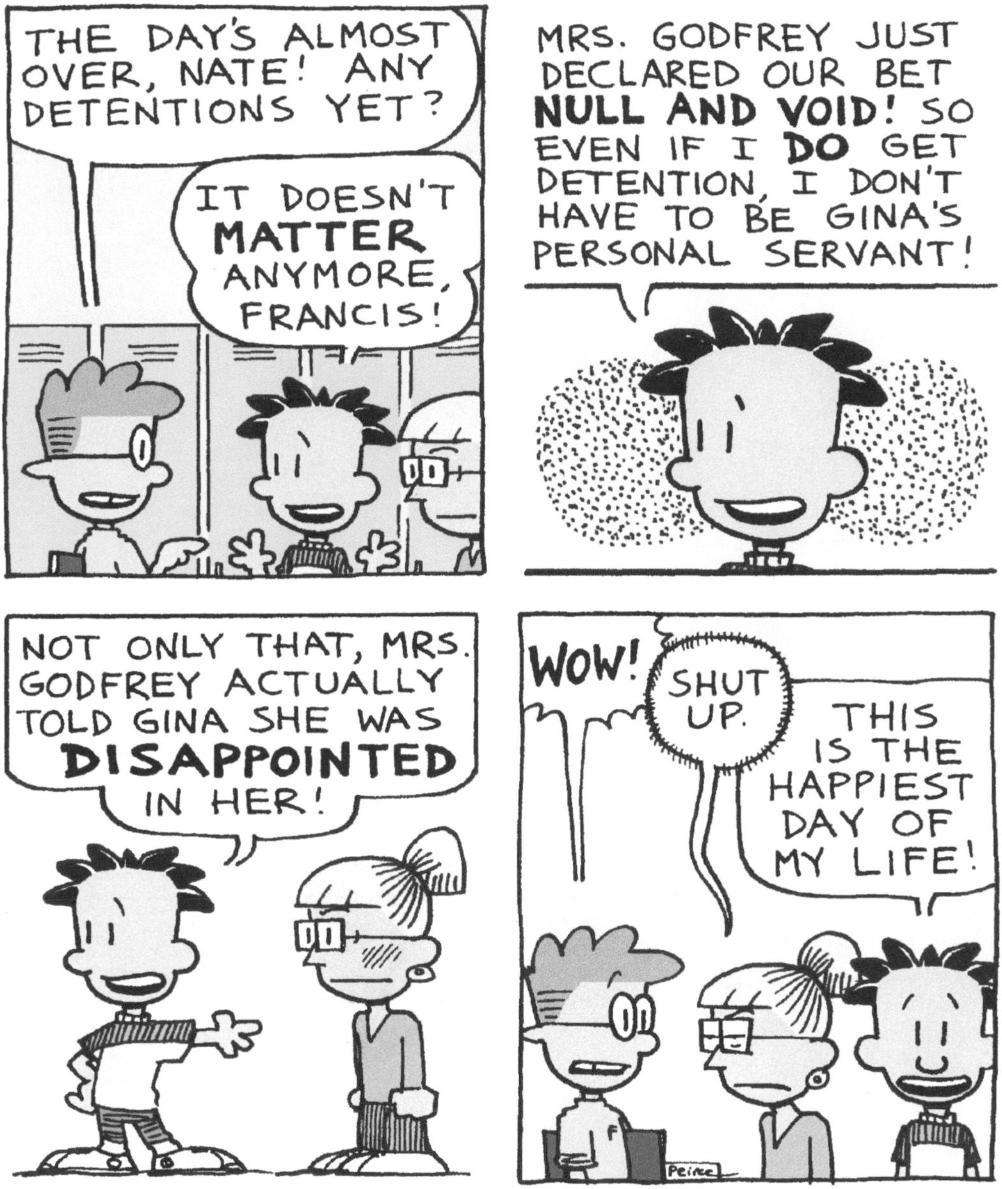
THE DAY'S ALMOST OVER, NATE! ANY DETENTIONS YET?
IT DOESN'T **MATTER** ANYMORE, FRANCIS!
MRS. GODFREY JUST DECLARED OUR BET **NULL AND VOID!** SO EVEN IF I **DO** GET DETENTION, I DON'T HAVE TO BE GINA'S PERSONAL SERVANT!
NOT ONLY THAT, MRS. GODFREY ACTUALLY TOLD GINA SHE WAS **DISAPPOINTED** IN HER!
WOW!
SHUT UP.
THIS IS THE HAPPIEST DAY OF MY LIFE!
Peirce

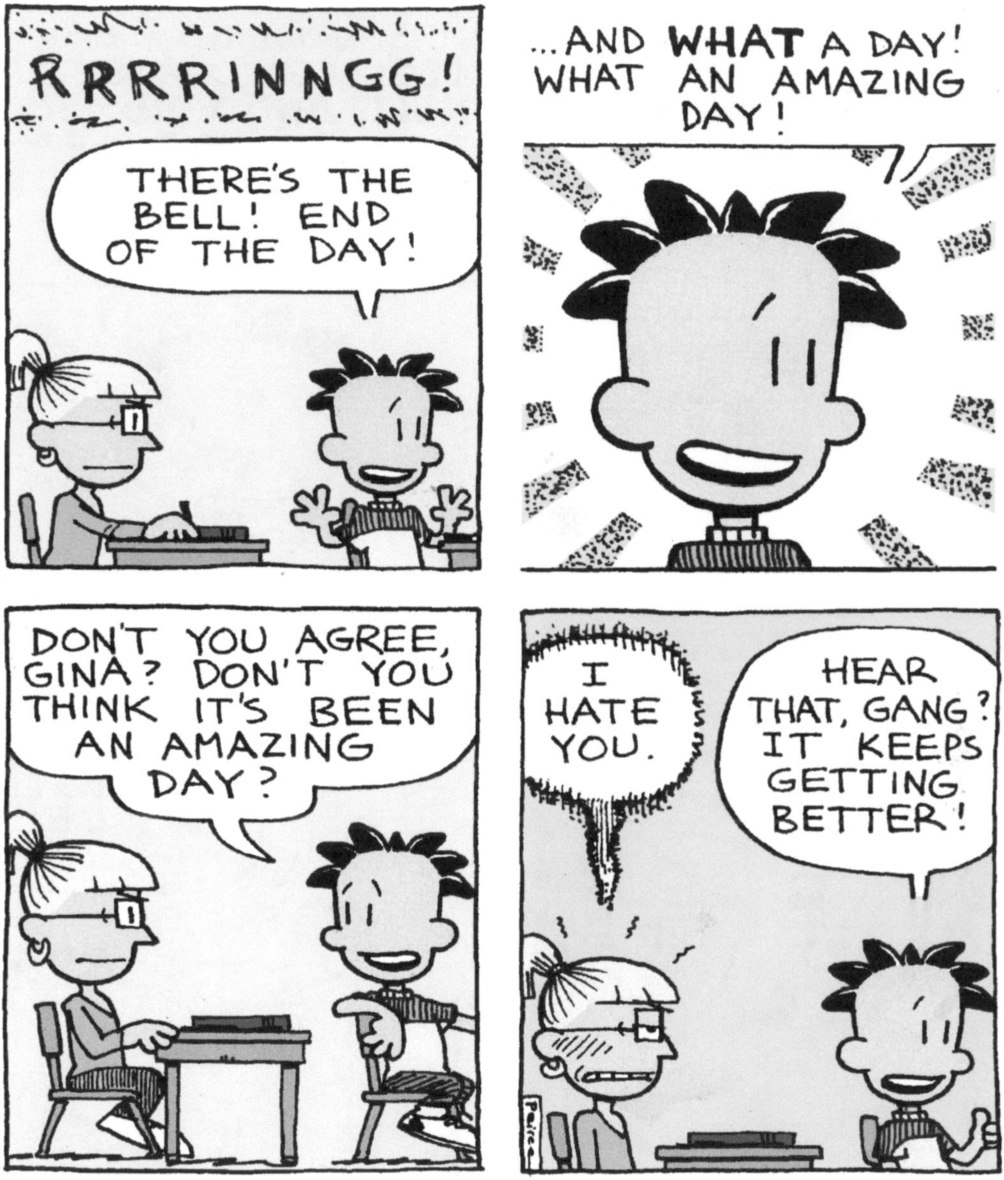
RRRRINNGG!
THERE'S THE BELL! END OF THE DAY!
...AND WHAT A DAY! WHAT AN AMAZING DAY!
DON'T YOU AGREE, GINA? DON'T YOU THINK IT'S BEEN AN AMAZING DAY?
I HATE YOU.
HEAR THAT, GANG? IT KEEPS GETTING BETTER!
Peirce

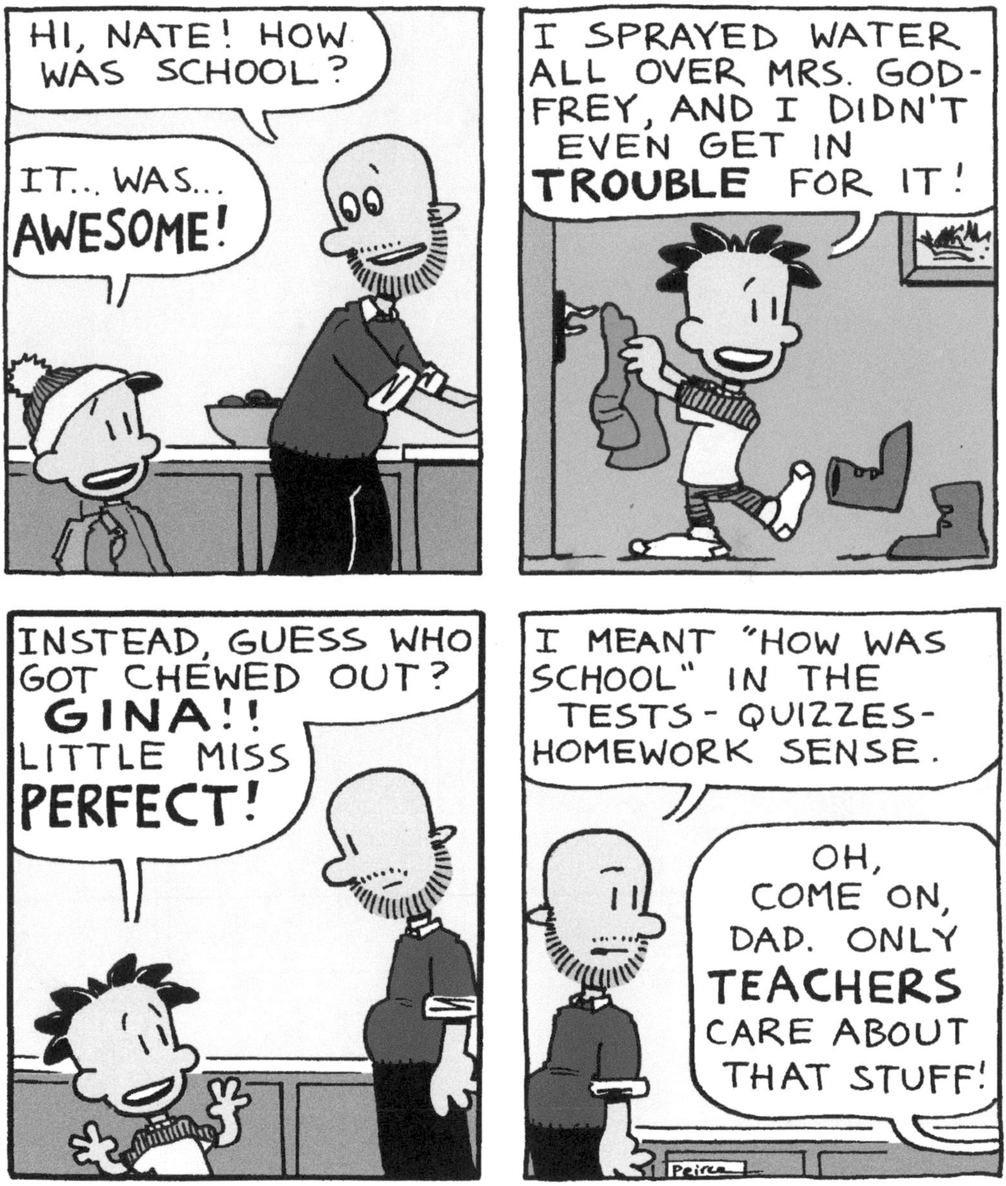
HI, NATE! HOW WAS SCHOOL?
IT... WAS... AWESOME!
I SPRAYED WATER ALL OVER MRS. GOD-FREY, AND I DIDN'T EVEN GET IN TROUBLE FOR IT!
INSTEAD, GUESS WHO GOT CHEWED OUT? GINA!! LITTLE MISS PERFECT!
I MEANT "HOW WAS SCHOOL" IN THE TESTS-QUIZZES-HOMEWORK SENSE.
OH, COME ON, DAD. ONLY TEACHERS CARE ABOUT THAT STUFF!
Peirce

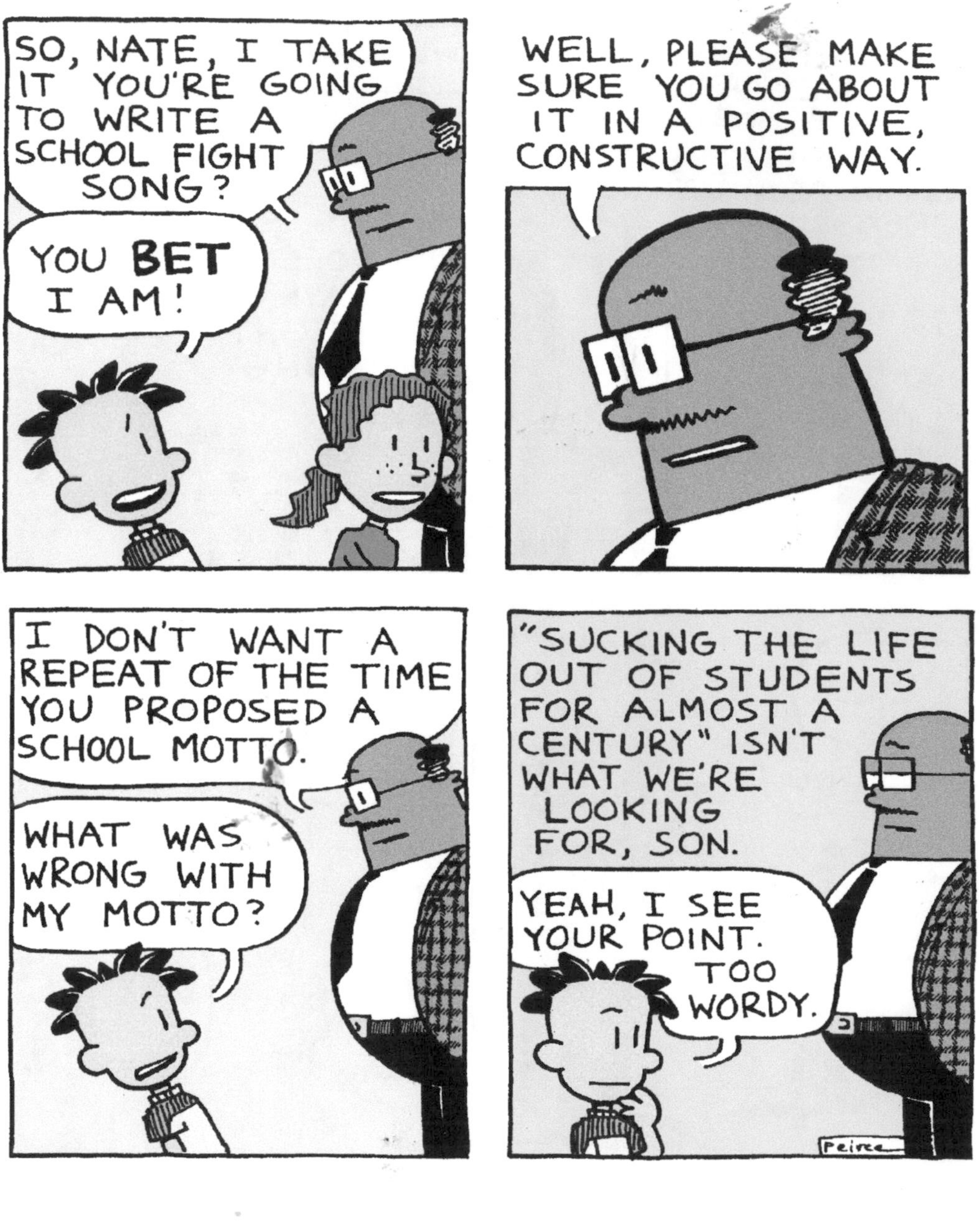
SO, NATE, I TAKE IT YOU'RE GOING TO WRITE A SCHOOL FIGHT SONG?
YOU **BET** I AM!
WELL, PLEASE MAKE SURE YOU GO ABOUT IT IN A POSITIVE, CONSTRUCTIVE WAY.
I DON'T WANT A REPEAT OF THE TIME YOU PROPOSED A SCHOOL MOTTO.
WHAT WAS WRONG WITH MY MOTTO?
"SUCKING THE LIFE OUT OF STUDENTS FOR ALMOST A CENTURY" ISN'T WHAT WE'RE LOOKING FOR, SON.
YEAH, I SEE YOUR POINT. TOO WORDY.
Peirce

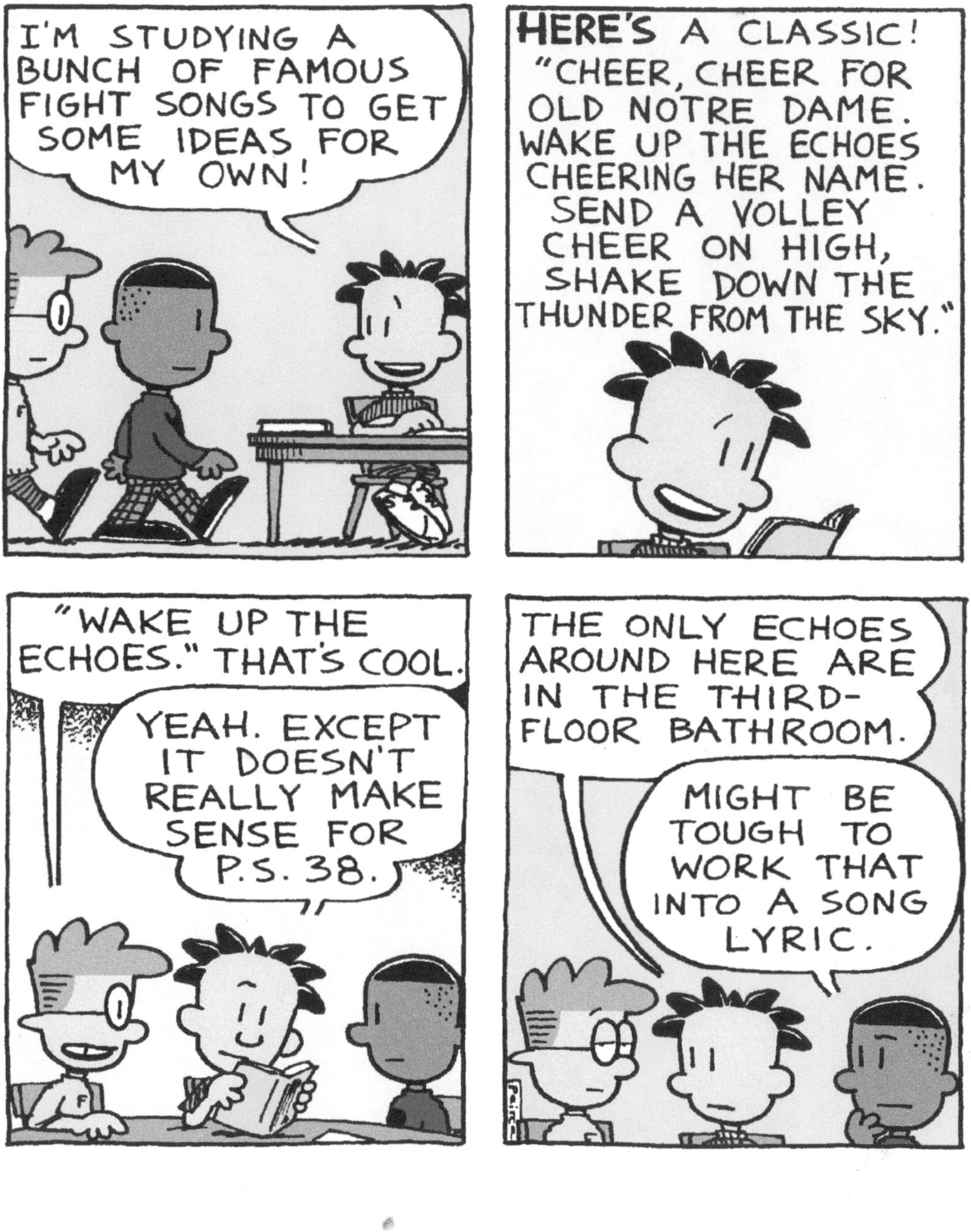
I'M STUDYING A BUNCH OF FAMOUS FIGHT SONGS TO GET SOME IDEAS FOR MY OWN!
HERE'S A CLASSIC! "CHEER, CHEER FOR OLD NOTRE DAME. WAKE UP THE ECHOES CHEERING HER NAME. SEND A VOLLEY CHEER ON HIGH, SHAKE DOWN THE THUNDER FROM THE SKY."
"WAKE UP THE ECHOES." THAT'S COOL.
YEAH. EXCEPT IT DOESN'T REALLY MAKE SENSE FOR P.S. 38.
THE ONLY ECHOES AROUND HERE ARE IN THE THIRD-FLOOR BATHROOM.
MIGHT BE TOUGH TO WORK THAT INTO A SONG LYRIC.
Peirce

IT'S **SHOCKING** THAT P.S. 38 DOESN'T HAVE A FIGHT SONG! IT'S COMPLETELY UNACCEPTABLE!

HAVING NO FIGHT SONG TELLS EVERY-BODY WE'RE A **SECOND-CLASS INSTITUTION!**

I THOUGHT WE WERE A SECOND-CLASS INSTITUTION BECAUSE THE **FRENCH FRIES** IN THE CAFETORIUM ARE ALWAYS **UNDERCOOKED!**

SOGGY FRIES ARE AN **OUT-RAGE!**

CHAD, LET'S TRY TO STAY ON TOPIC.

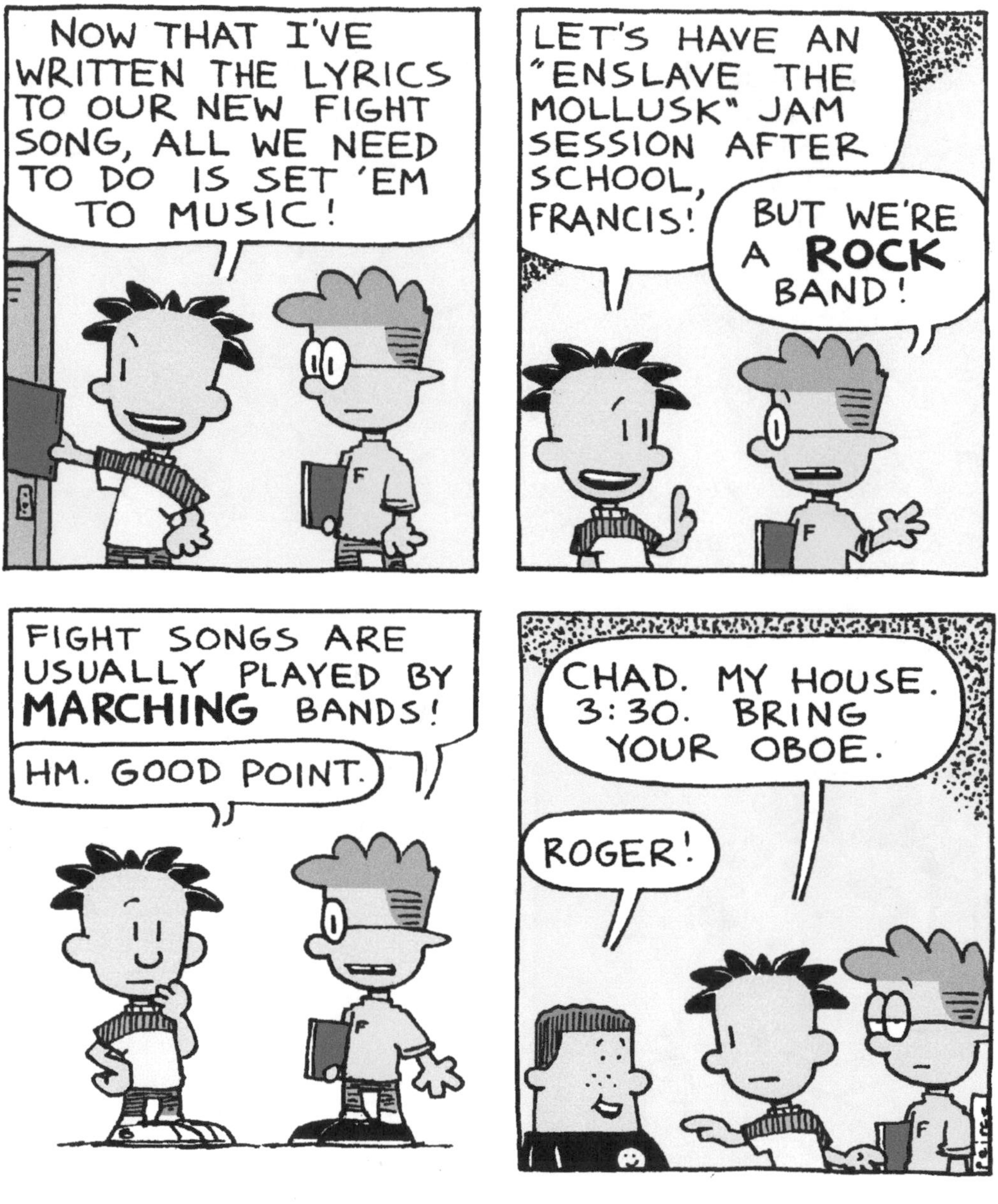
NOW THAT I'VE WRITTEN THE LYRICS TO OUR NEW FIGHT SONG, ALL WE NEED TO DO IS SET 'EM TO MUSIC!
LET'S HAVE AN "ENSLAVE THE MOLLUSK" JAM SESSION AFTER SCHOOL, FRANCIS!
BUT WE'RE A **ROCK** BAND!
FIGHT SONGS ARE USUALLY PLAYED BY **MARCHING** BANDS!
HM. GOOD POINT.
CHAD. MY HOUSE. 3:30. BRING YOUR OBOE.
ROGER!

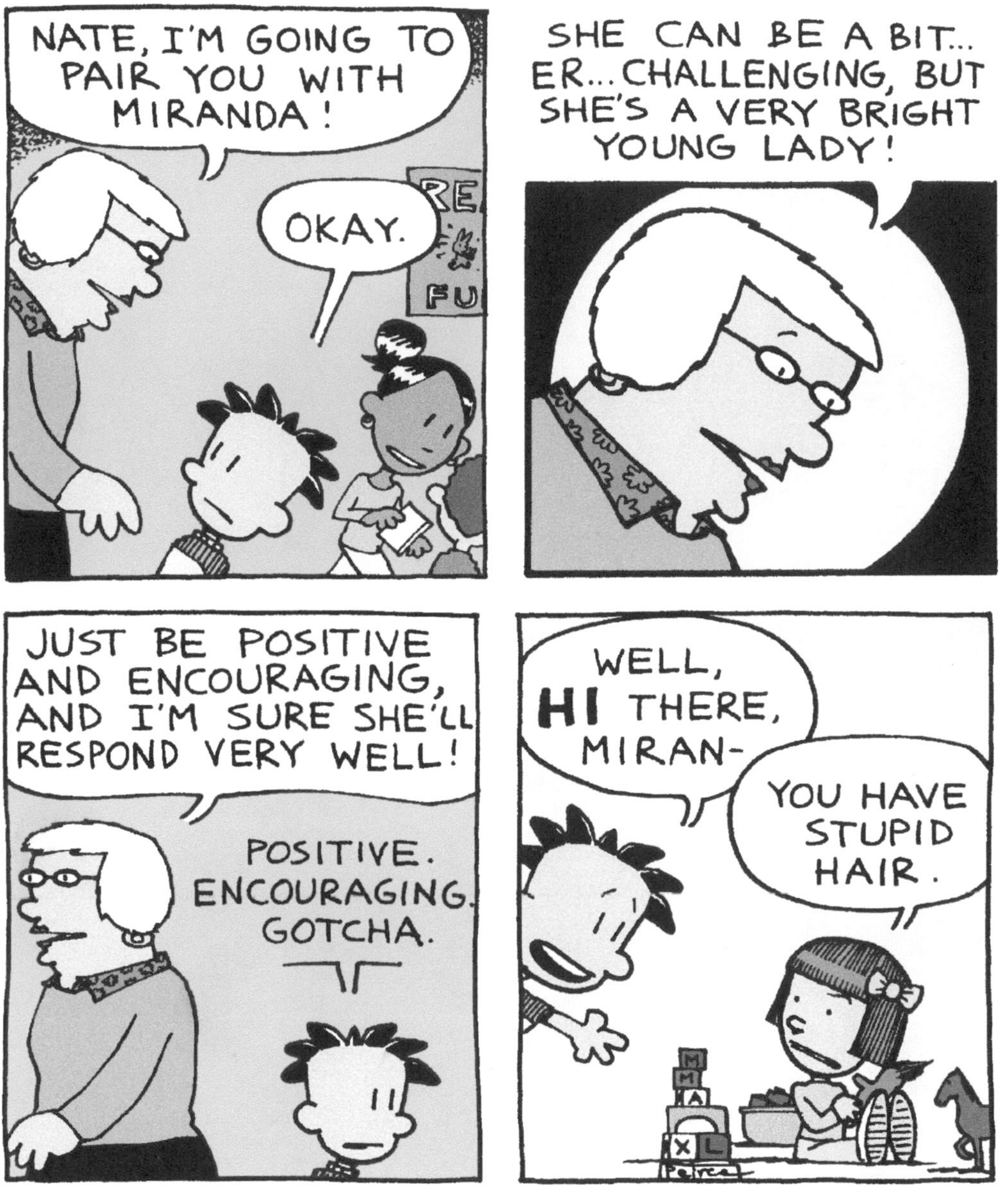
NATE, I'M GOING TO PAIR YOU WITH MIRANDA!
OKAY.
SHE CAN BE A BIT... ER...CHALLENGING, BUT SHE'S A VERY BRIGHT YOUNG LADY!
JUST BE POSITIVE AND ENCOURAGING, AND I'M SURE SHE'LL RESPOND VERY WELL!
POSITIVE. ENCOURAGING. GOTCHA.
WELL, **HI** THERE, MIRAN-
YOU HAVE STUPID HAIR.

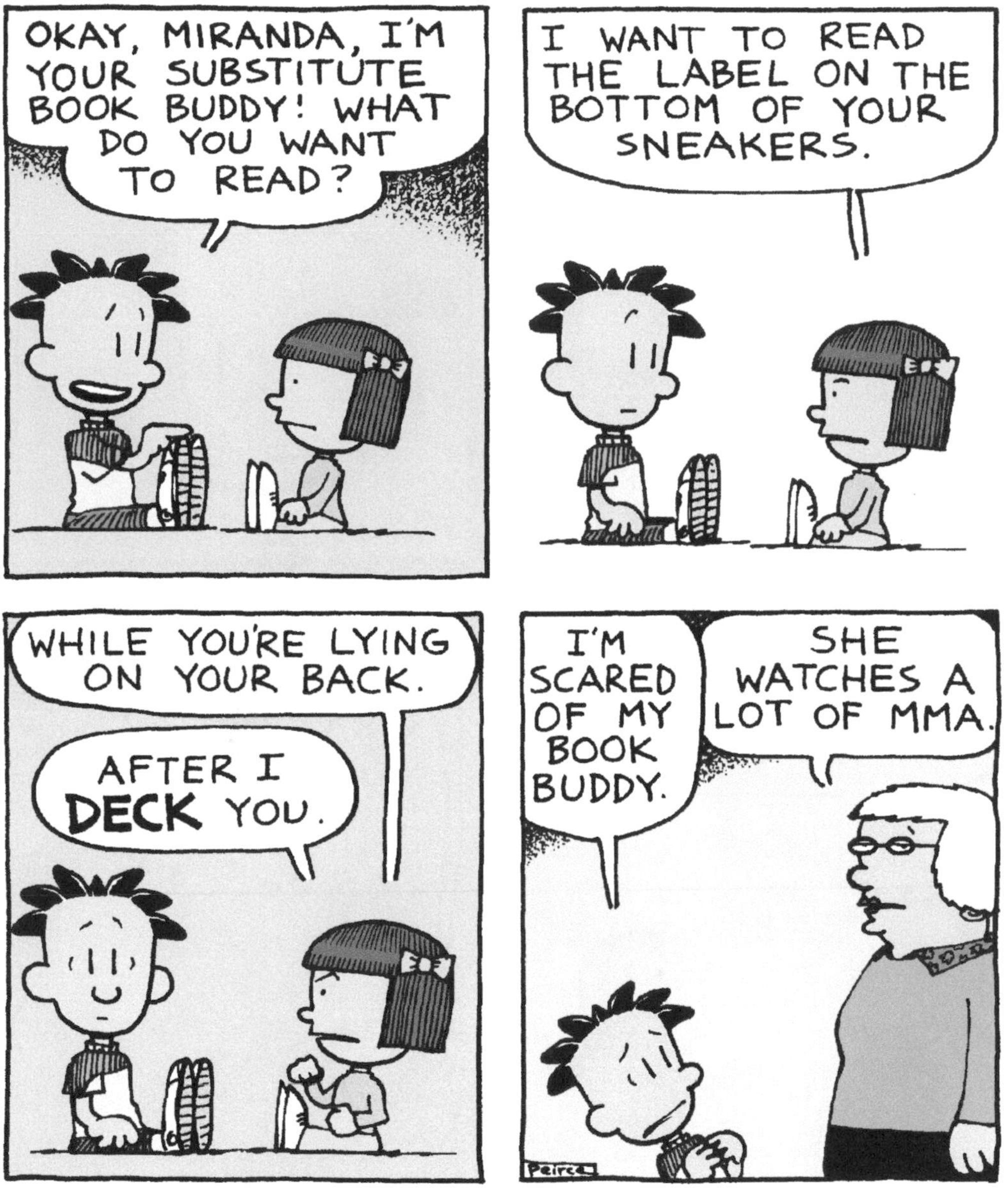
OKAY, MIRANDA, I'M YOUR SUBSTITUTE BOOK BUDDY! WHAT DO YOU WANT TO READ?
I WANT TO READ THE LABEL ON THE BOTTOM OF YOUR SNEAKERS.
WHILE YOU'RE LYING ON YOUR BACK.
AFTER I DECK YOU.
I'M SCARED OF MY BOOK BUDDY.
SHE WATCHES A LOT OF MMA.
Peirce

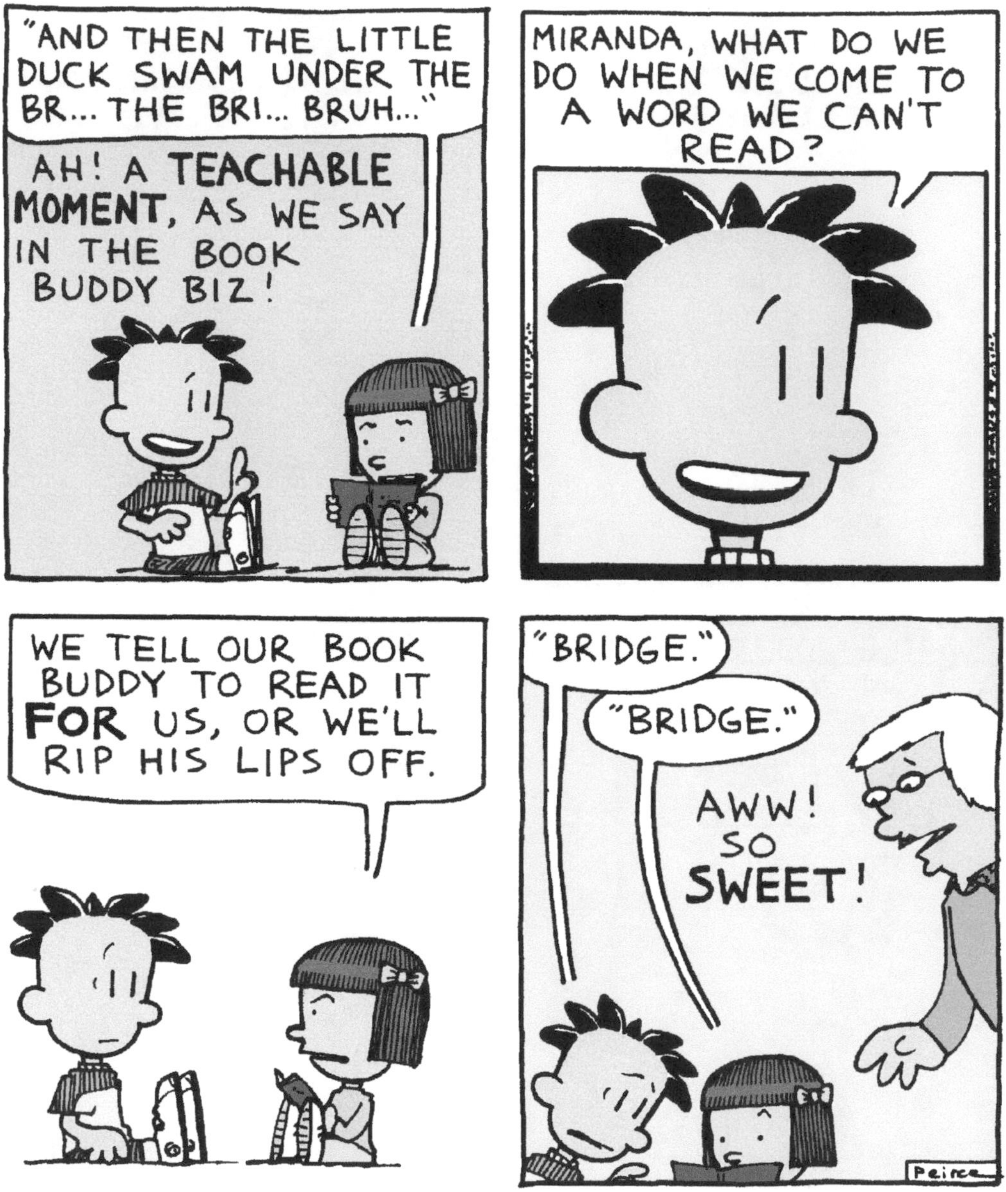
"AND THEN THE LITTLE DUCK SWAM UNDER THE BR... THE BRI... BRUH..."
AH! A **TEACHABLE MOMENT**, AS WE SAY IN THE BOOK BUDDY BIZ!
MIRANDA, WHAT DO WE DO WHEN WE COME TO A WORD WE CAN'T READ?
WE TELL OUR BOOK BUDDY TO READ IT **FOR** US, OR WE'LL RIP HIS LIPS OFF.
"BRIDGE."
"BRIDGE."
AWW! SO **SWEET**!
Peirce

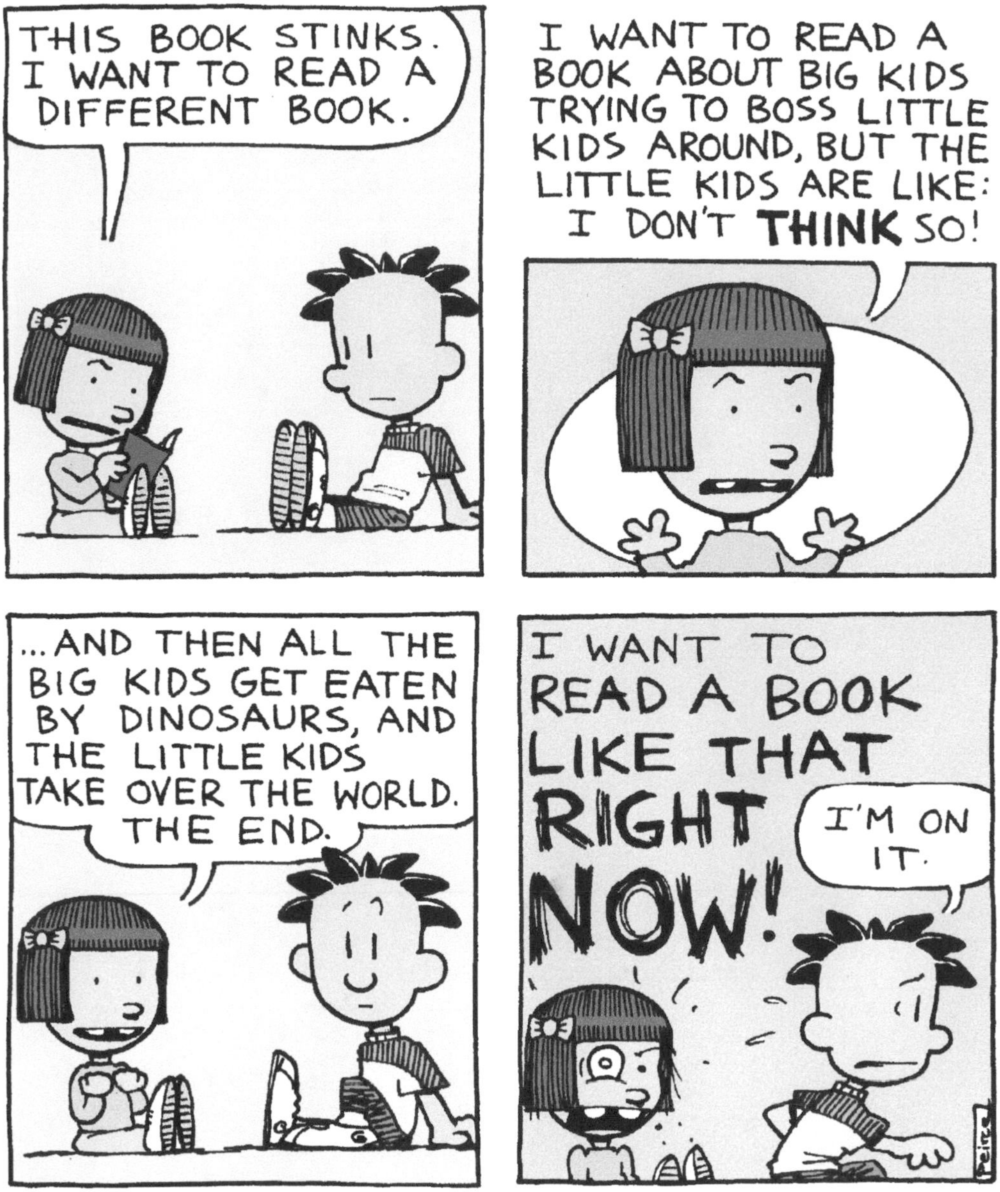
THIS BOOK STINKS. I WANT TO READ A DIFFERENT BOOK.
I WANT TO READ A BOOK ABOUT BIG KIDS TRYING TO BOSS LITTLE KIDS AROUND, BUT THE LITTLE KIDS ARE LIKE: I DON'T THINK SO!
...AND THEN ALL THE BIG KIDS GET EATEN BY DINOSAURS, AND THE LITTLE KIDS TAKE OVER THE WORLD. THE END.
I WANT TO READ A BOOK LIKE THAT RIGHT NOW!
I'M ON IT.
Peirce

I HATE BOOK BUDDY TIME.

NOW, NOW, MIRANDA!

WE'LL NEVER FIND OUT WHAT HAPPENS TO BIPPITY BUNNY WITH **THAT** ATTITUDE! KEEP READING!

SIGH

"BIPPITY WAVED GOODBYE TO GRANNY GRUMBLE AND STARTED ON HIS WAY. SOON HE MET A... A..."

"PEDDLER"

A PEDAL IS PART OF A BICYCLE! SO BIPPITY MUST HAVE MET SOMEONE RIDING A **BIKE!**

BUT...

THAT'S NOT WHAT IT MEANS!

IF SOMEONE WAS RIDING A **BIKE**, IT WOULD BE SPELLED P-E-D-A-L-E-R! A **PEDDLER** IS SOMEBODY WHO **SELLS** STUFF!

YOU'RE EVEN STUPIDER THAN YOU LOOK.

WHEN I WAS IN FIRST GRADE, WE WERE **AFRAID** OF SIXTH-GRADERS.

I **LIKE** BOOK BUDDY TIME!

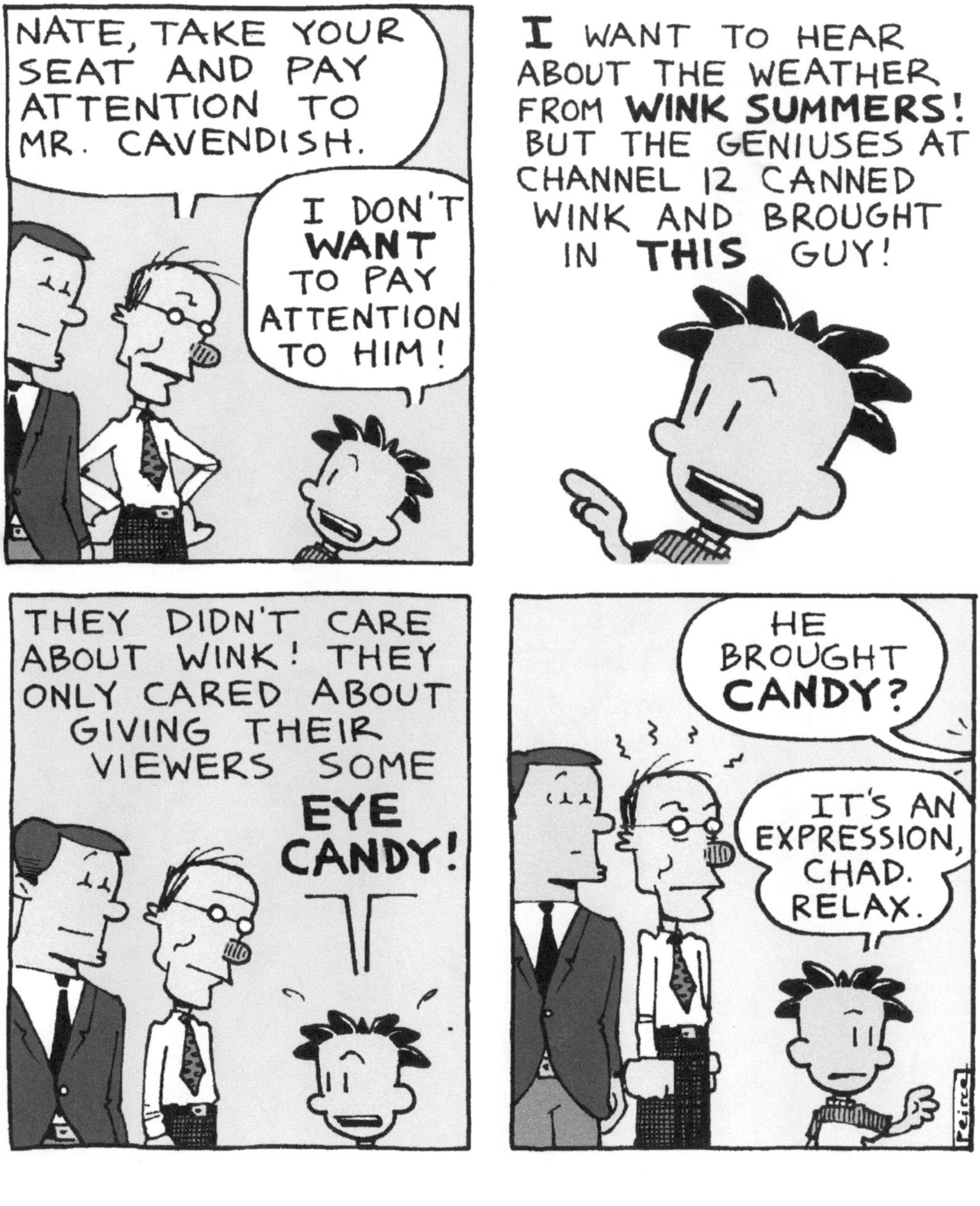
NATE, TAKE YOUR SEAT AND PAY ATTENTION TO MR. CAVENDISH.
I DON'T WANT TO PAY ATTENTION TO HIM!
I WANT TO HEAR ABOUT THE WEATHER FROM WINK SUMMERS! BUT THE GENIUSES AT CHANNEL 12 CANNED WINK AND BROUGHT IN THIS GUY!
THEY DIDN'T CARE ABOUT WINK! THEY ONLY CARED ABOUT GIVING THEIR VIEWERS SOME EYE CANDY!
HE BROUGHT CANDY?
IT'S AN EXPRESSION, CHAD. RELAX.
Peirce

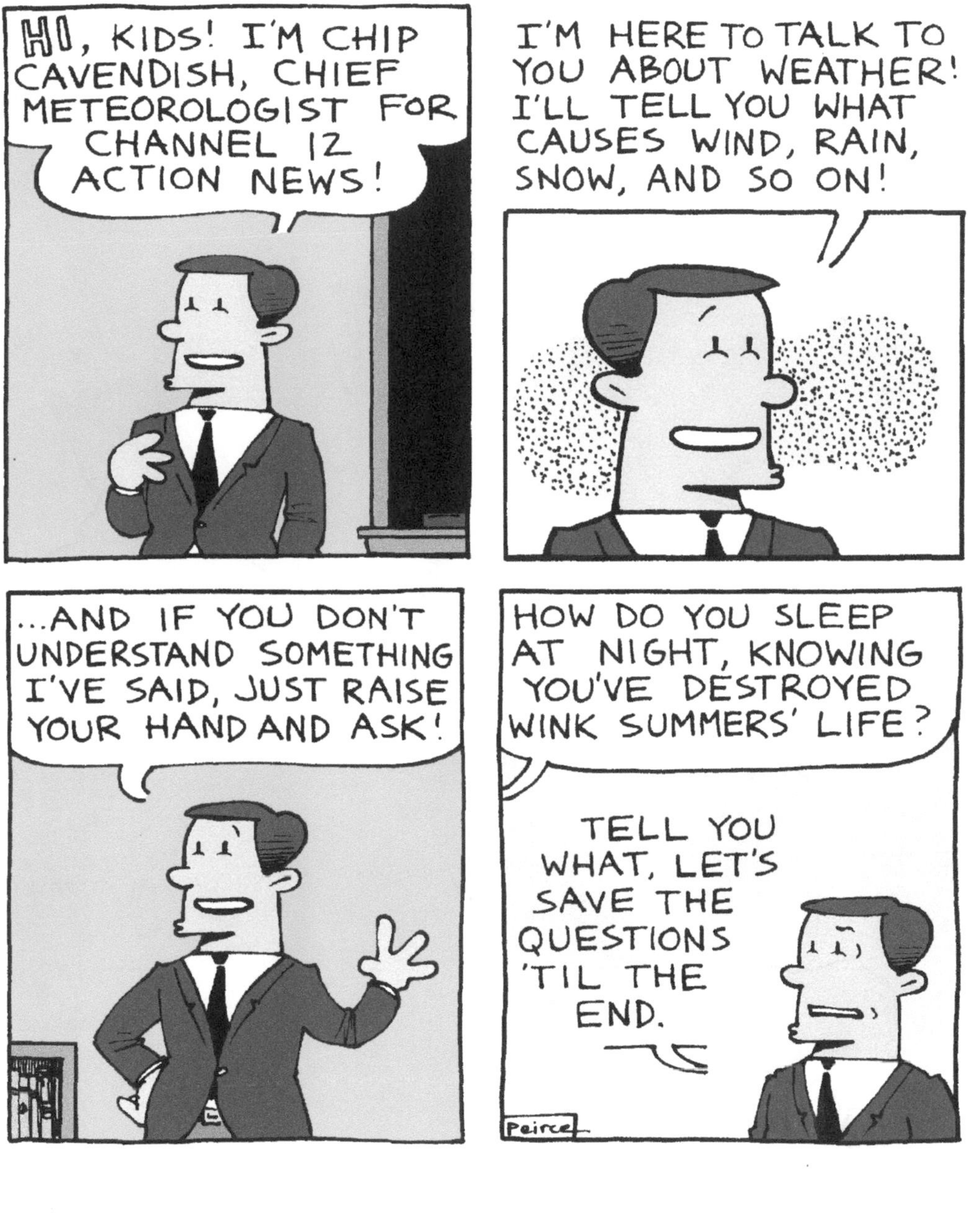
HI, KIDS! I'M CHIP CAVENDISH, CHIEF METEOROLOGIST FOR CHANNEL 12 ACTION NEWS!
I'M HERE TO TALK TO YOU ABOUT WEATHER! I'LL TELL YOU WHAT CAUSES WIND, RAIN, SNOW, AND SO ON!
...AND IF YOU DON'T UNDERSTAND SOMETHING I'VE SAID, JUST RAISE YOUR HAND AND ASK!
HOW DO YOU SLEEP AT NIGHT, KNOWING YOU'VE DESTROYED WINK SUMMERS' LIFE?
TELL YOU WHAT, LET'S SAVE THE QUESTIONS 'TIL THE END.
Peirce

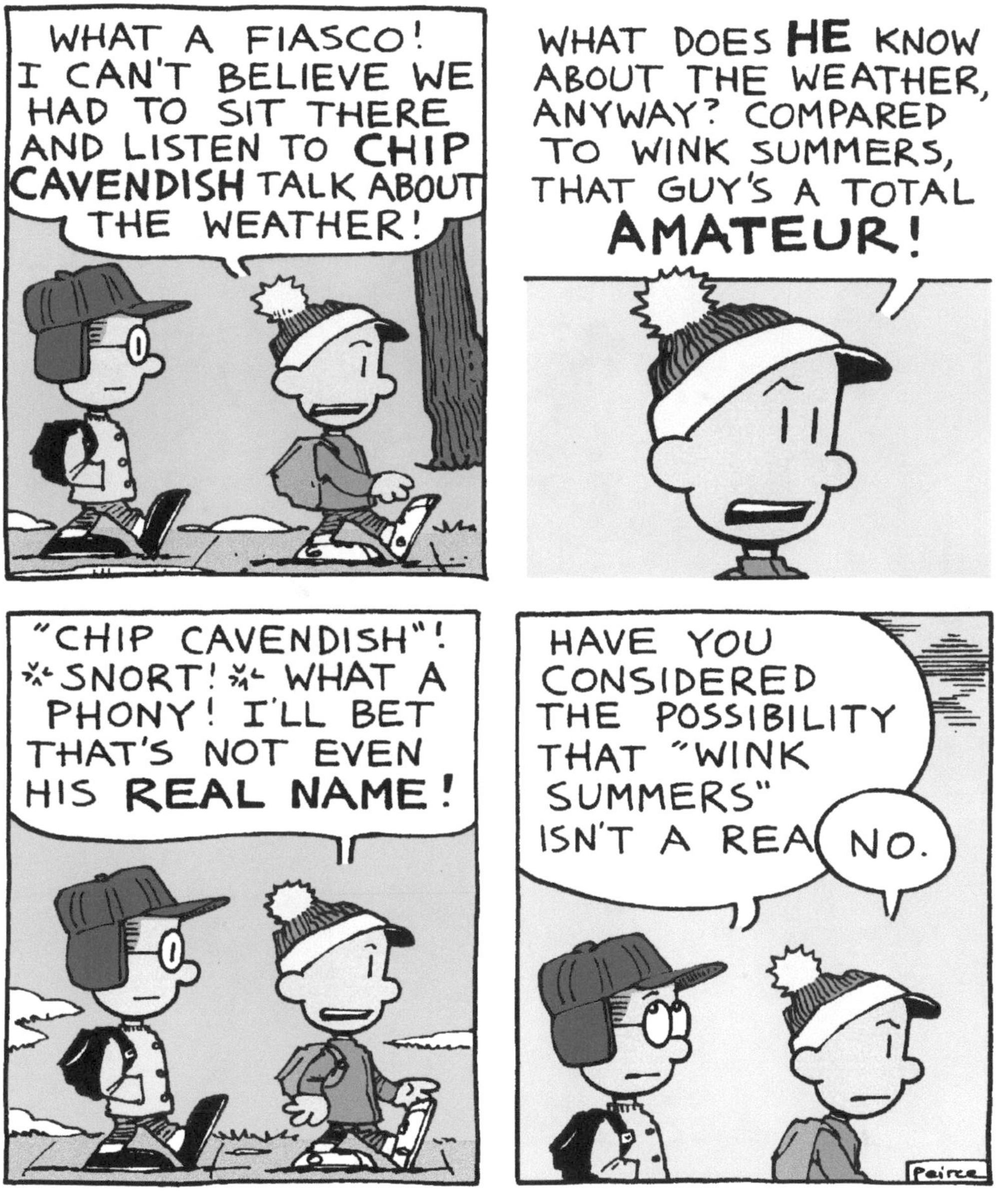
WHAT A FIASCO! I CAN'T BELIEVE WE HAD TO SIT THERE AND LISTEN TO CHIP CAVENDISH TALK ABOUT THE WEATHER!
WHAT DOES HE KNOW ABOUT THE WEATHER, ANYWAY? COMPARED TO WINK SUMMERS, THAT GUY'S A TOTAL AMATEUR!
"CHIP CAVENDISH"! SNORT! WHAT A PHONY! I'LL BET THAT'S NOT EVEN HIS REAL NAME!
HAVE YOU CONSIDERED THE POSSIBILITY THAT "WINK SUMMERS" ISN'T A REA
NO.
Peirce

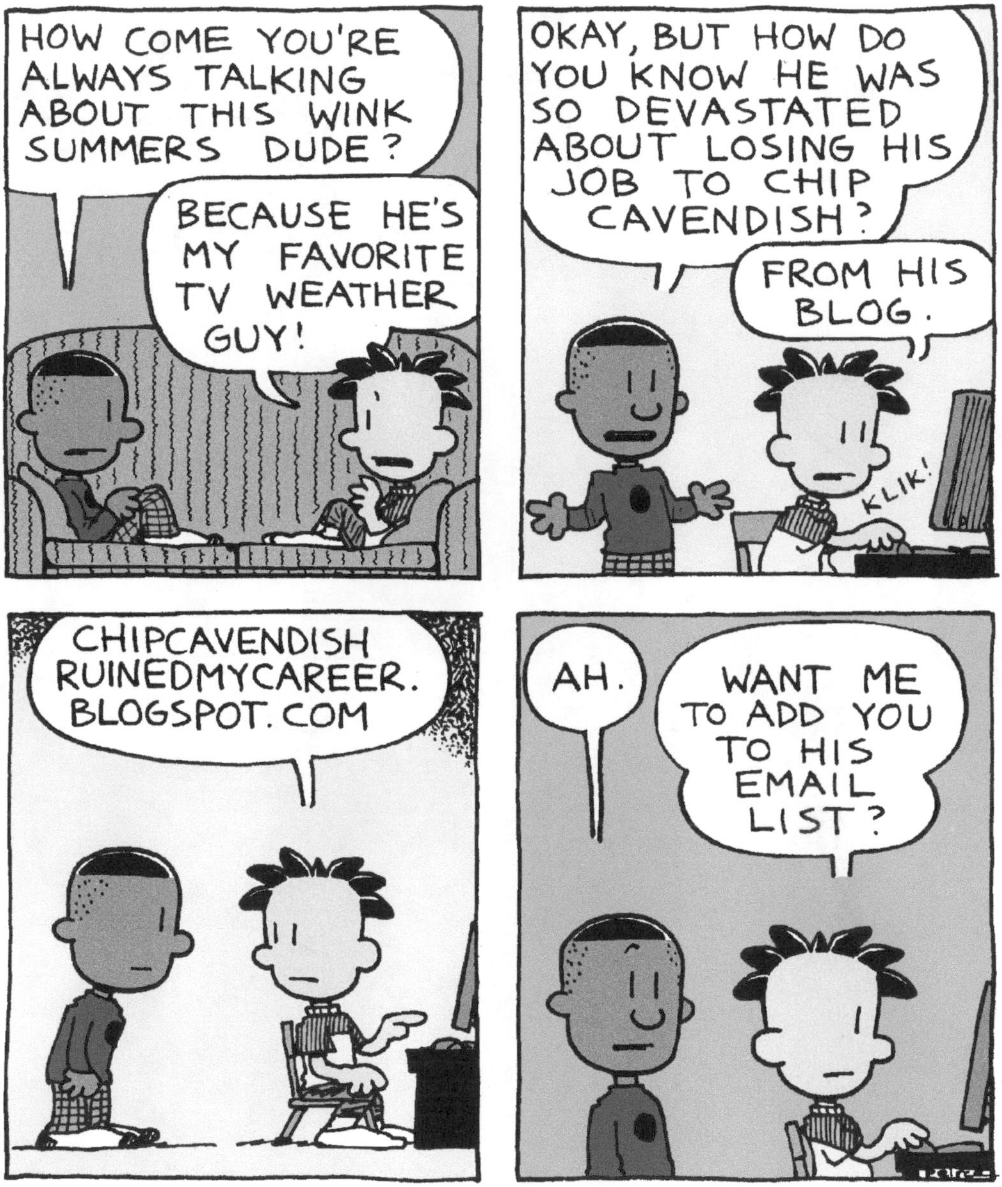
HOW COME YOU'RE ALWAYS TALKING ABOUT THIS WINK SUMMERS DUDE?
BECAUSE HE'S MY FAVORITE TV WEATHER GUY!
OKAY, BUT HOW DO YOU KNOW HE WAS SO DEVASTATED ABOUT LOSING HIS JOB TO CHIP CAVENDISH?
FROM HIS BLOG.
KLIK!
CHIPCAVENDISH RUINEDMYCAREER. BLOGSPOT.COM
AH.
WANT ME TO ADD YOU TO HIS EMAIL LIST?

TRAGICALLY, THOUGH, MY DREAMS WERE DASHED. MY PARENTS THOUGHT METEOROLOGY WAS A FRIVOLOUS PURSUIT.

HI, LADY. WILL YOU SIGN MY PETITION TO GET WINK SUMMERS REINSTATED AS CHANNEL 12'S CHIEF METEOROLOGIST?

WINK SUMMERS?

WINK SUMMERS SAID MY WEDDING DAY WOULD BE WARM AND SUNNY!

DO YOU KNOW WHAT IT DID? IT HAILED!

YOU'RE NOT GOING TO SIGN MY PETITION, ARE YOU?

MY AUNT PATTY GOT A CONCUSSION!

...AND I'M HOPING IF ENOUGH PEOPLE SIGN THIS PETITION, CHANNEL 12 WILL GIVE WINK SUMMERS HIS JOB BACK!

BUT THEN WHAT WILL HAPPEN TO THE YOUNG FELLOW WHO **REPLACED** HIM?

CHIP CAVENDISH? WHO **CARES**?

HE'S NOT THERE BECAUSE HE'S A GOOD METEOROLOGIST! HE'S THERE BECAUSE HE LOOKS LIKE A J. CREW MODEL!

EXACTLY.

ROWR!

SNAP!

SNAP!

MRS. O'MALLEY! HE**LLO**? FOCUS!

WELCOME TO CHANNEL 12! HOW MAY I HELP YOU?

CAN YOU GIVE THIS TO THE STATION MANAGER?

IT'S A PETITION TO GET WINK SUMMERS HIS JOB BACK AS CHIEF METEOROLOGIST!

MY GOODNESS, WHAT A LOT OF SIGNATURES!

YUP! FIVE HUNDRED PEOPLE!

...480 OF WHOM HAVE IDENTICAL HAND-WRITING.

IT'S A VERY CLOSE NEIGH-BORHOOD.

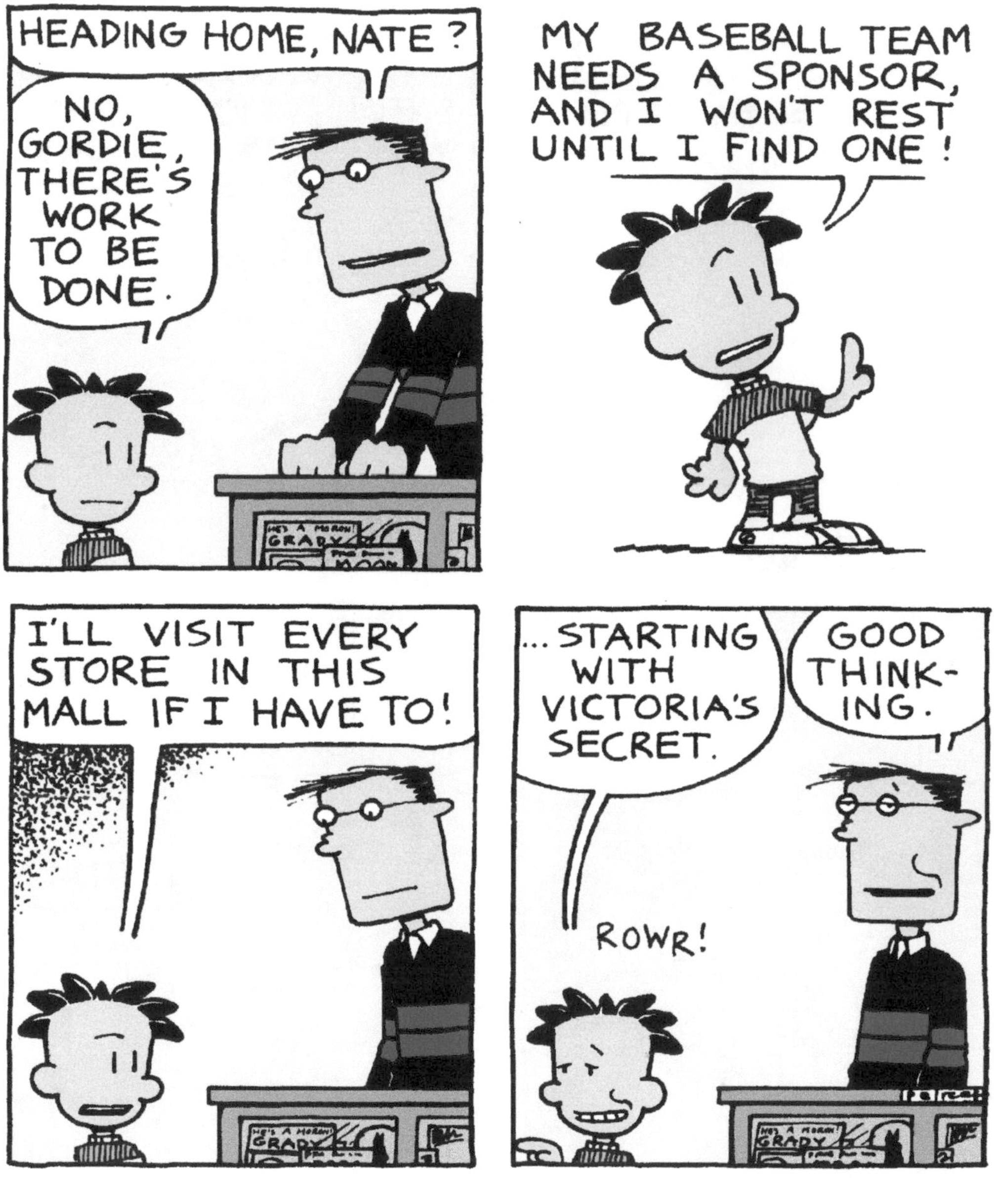
HEADING HOME, NATE?
NO, GORDIE, THERE'S WORK TO BE DONE.
MY BASEBALL TEAM NEEDS A SPONSOR, AND I WON'T REST UNTIL I FIND ONE!
I'LL VISIT EVERY STORE IN THIS MALL IF I HAVE TO!
...STARTING WITH VICTORIA'S SECRET.
ROWR!
GOOD THINK-ING.

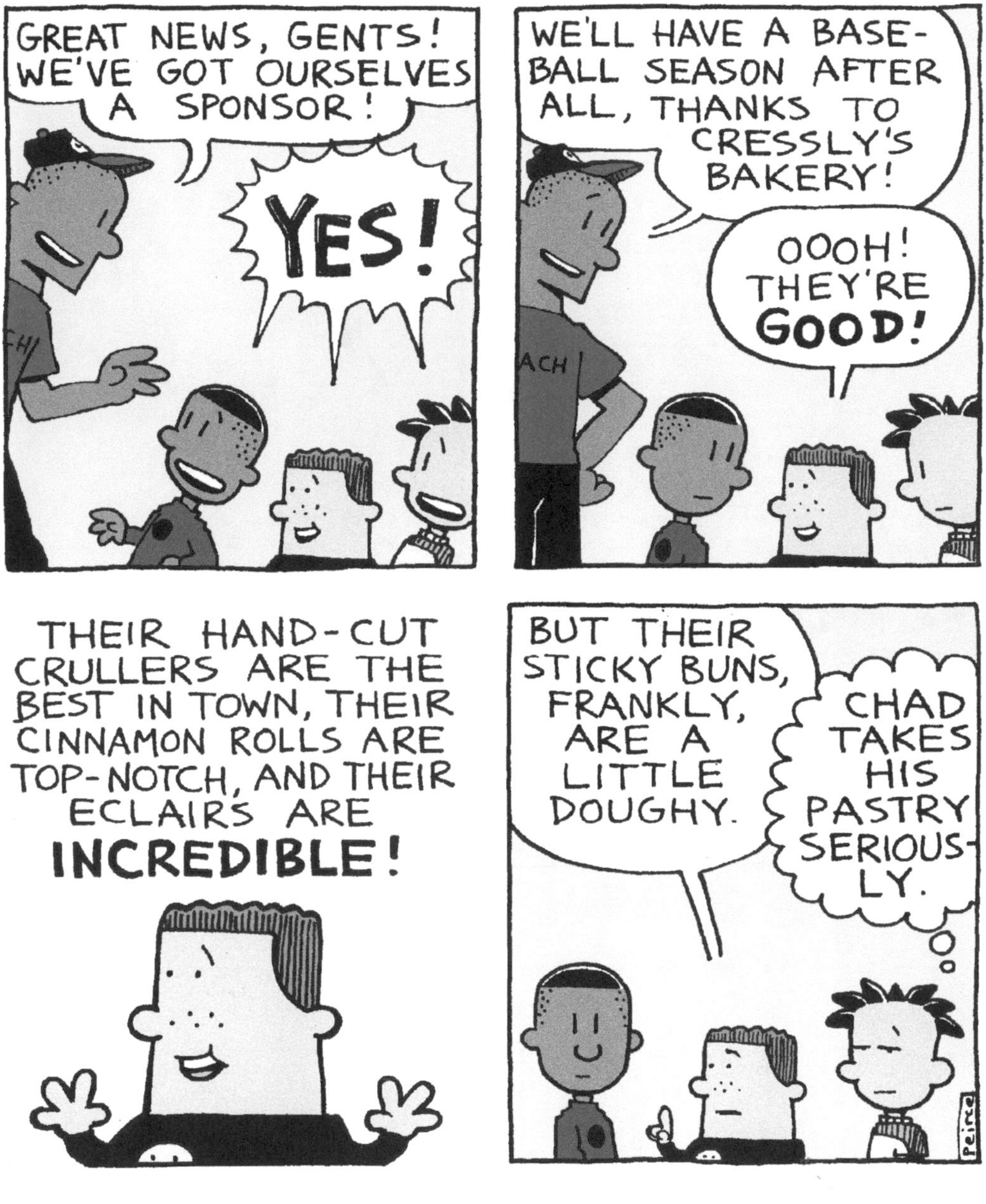
GREAT NEWS, GENTS! WE'VE GOT OURSELVES A SPONSOR!
YES!
WE'LL HAVE A BASE-BALL SEASON AFTER ALL, THANKS TO CRESSLY'S BAKERY!
OOOH! THEY'RE GOOD!
THEIR HAND-CUT CRULLERS ARE THE BEST IN TOWN, THEIR CINNAMON ROLLS ARE TOP-NOTCH, AND THEIR ECLAIRS ARE INCREDIBLE!
BUT THEIR STICKY BUNS, FRANKLY, ARE A LITTLE DOUGHY.
CHAD TAKES HIS PASTRY SERIOUS-LY.
Peirce

WAIT A MINUTE, KIM! HOW COME YOU'RE PLAYING BASEBALL? GIRLS PLAY **SOFTBALL!**

THERE **IS** NO SOFTBALL.

NOT ENOUGH GIRLS SIGNED UP, SO THE LEAGUE DISBANDED AND I SWITCHED TO BASEBALL.

SO NOW WE'RE TEAMMATES.

YEAH, THAT'S... THAT'S...

INCREDIBLY ROMANTIC.

NO!

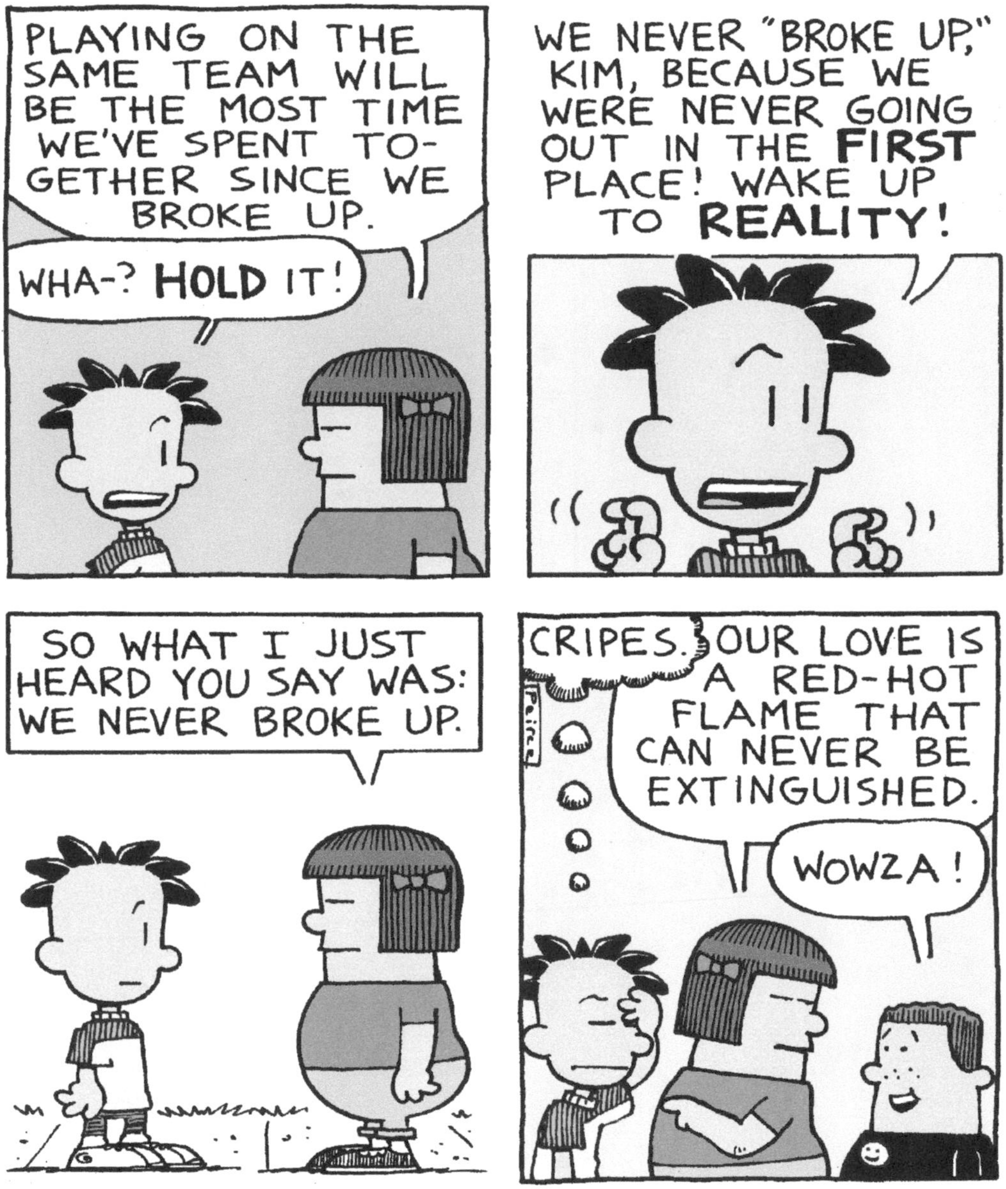
PLAYING ON THE SAME TEAM WILL BE THE MOST TIME WE'VE SPENT TO-GETHER SINCE WE BROKE UP.
WHA-? **HOLD** IT!
WE NEVER "BROKE UP," KIM, BECAUSE WE WERE NEVER GOING OUT IN THE **FIRST** PLACE! WAKE UP TO **REALITY**!
SO WHAT I JUST HEARD YOU SAY WAS: WE NEVER BROKE UP.
CRIPES.
OUR LOVE IS A RED-HOT FLAME THAT CAN NEVER BE EXTINGUISHED.
WOWZA!
Peirce

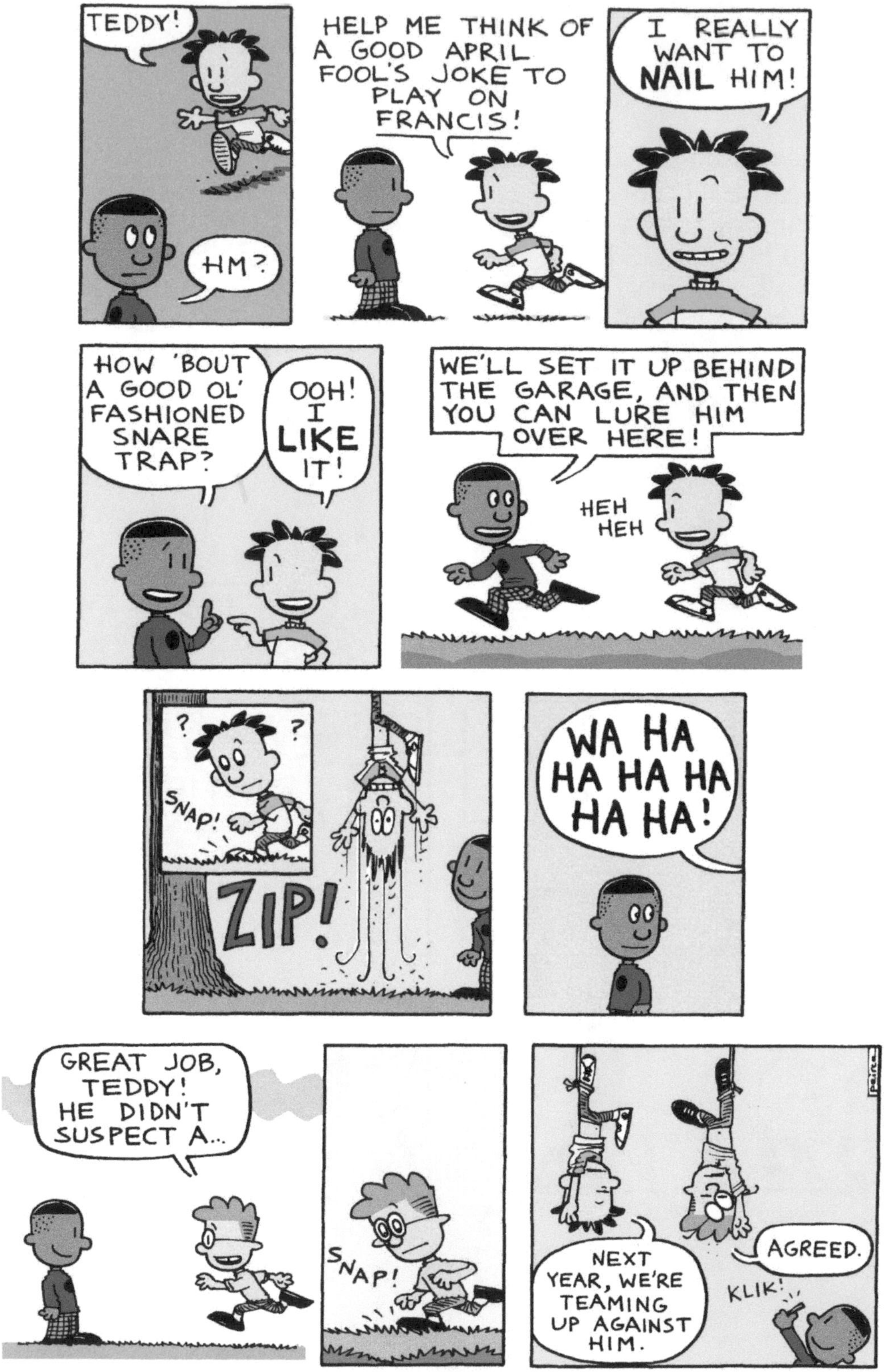
TEDDY!
HM?
HELP ME THINK OF A GOOD APRIL FOOL'S JOKE TO PLAY ON FRANCIS!
I REALLY WANT TO NAIL HIM!
HOW 'BOUT A GOOD OL' FASHIONED SNARE TRAP?
OOH! I LIKE IT!
WE'LL SET IT UP BEHIND THE GARAGE, AND THEN YOU CAN LURE HIM OVER HERE!
HEH HEH
? ?
SNAP!
ZIP!
WA HA HA HA HA HA HA!
GREAT JOB, TEDDY! HE DIDN'T SUSPECT A...
SNAP!
NEXT YEAR, WE'RE TEAMING UP AGAINST HIM.
AGREED.
KLIK!

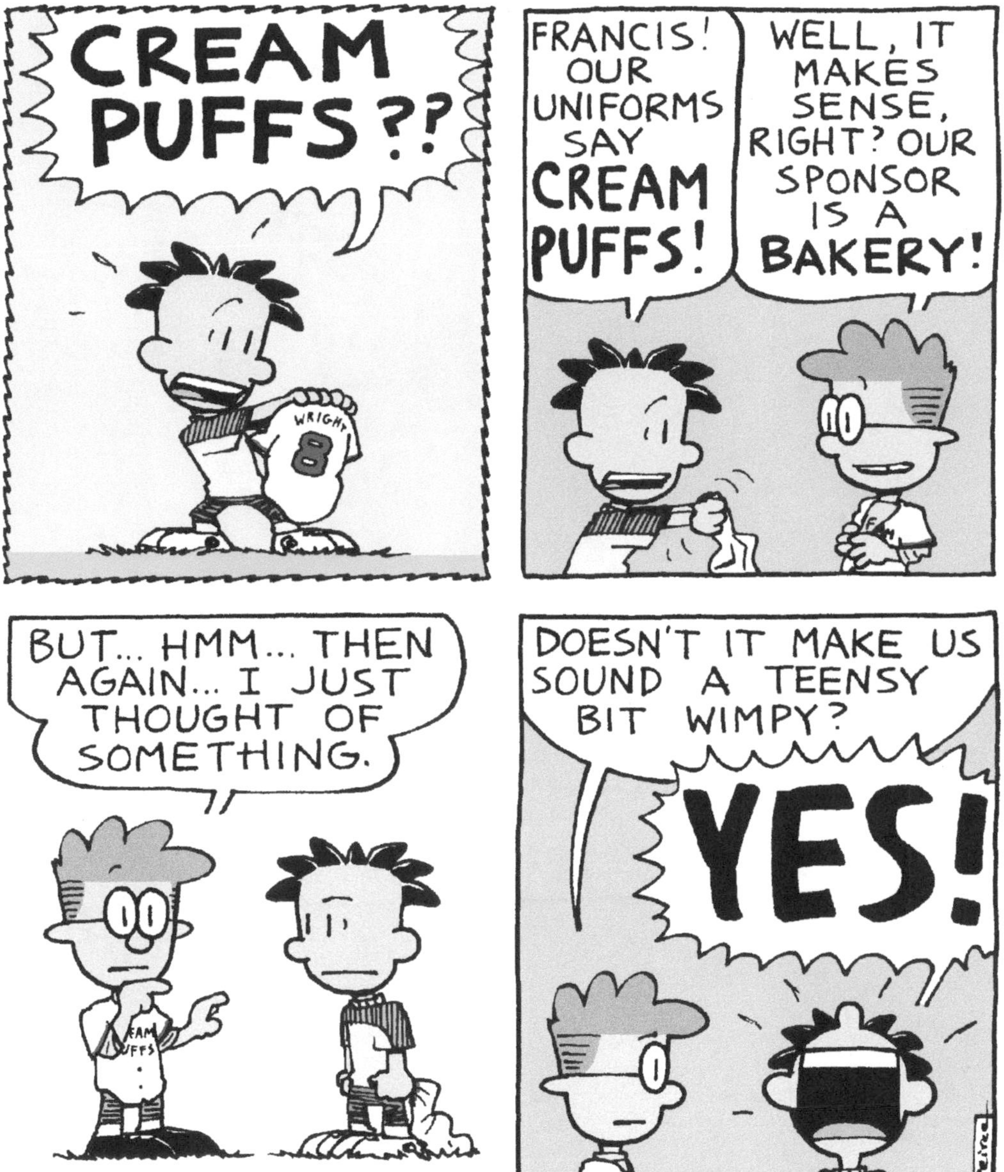
CREAM PUFFS??
FRANCIS! OUR UNIFORMS SAY CREAM PUFFS!
WELL, IT MAKES SENSE, RIGHT? OUR SPONSOR IS A BAKERY!
BUT... HMM... THEN AGAIN... I JUST THOUGHT OF SOMETHING.
DOESN'T IT MAKE US SOUND A TEENSY BIT WIMPY?
YES!

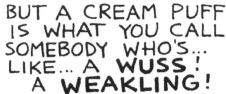

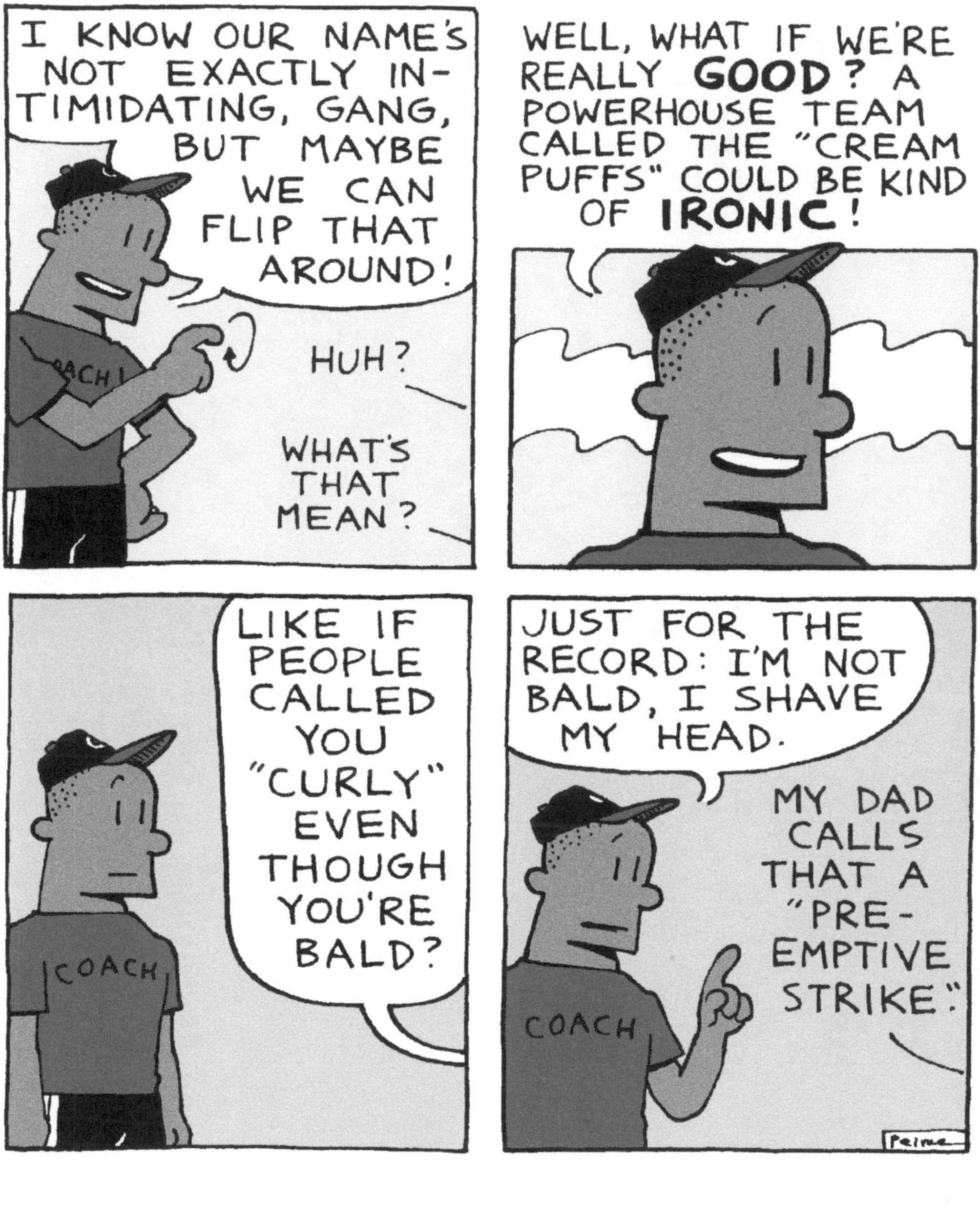
I KNOW OUR NAME'S NOT EXACTLY INTIMIDATING, GANG, BUT MAYBE WE CAN FLIP THAT AROUND!
COACH
HUH?
WHAT'S THAT MEAN?
WELL, WHAT IF WE'RE REALLY GOOD? A POWERHOUSE TEAM CALLED THE "CREAM PUFFS" COULD BE KIND OF IRONIC!
LIKE IF PEOPLE CALLED YOU "CURLY" EVEN THOUGH YOU'RE BALD?
COACH
JUST FOR THE RECORD: I'M NOT BALD, I SHAVE MY HEAD.
MY DAD CALLS THAT A "PRE-EMPTIVE STRIKE."
COACH
Peirce

MY LIFE IS RUINED.

HM? WHY'S THAT, BUD?

MY **BASEBALL TEAM!** WE'RE SPONSORED BY CRESSLY'S BAKERY, AND YOU KNOW WHAT THEY PUT ON OUR UNIFORMS?

NOT "CRESSLY'S BAKERY"?

NO! **"CREAM PUFFS"!** RIGHT ACROSS OUR CHESTS IT SAYS **"CREAM PUFFS"!**

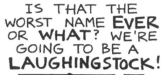

IS THAT THE WORST NAME **EVER** OR **WHAT?** WE'RE GOING TO BE A **LAUGHINGSTOCK!**

ALL THE **OTHER** TEAMS HAVE **REAL** NAMES LIKE "AL'S AUTO GLASS" AND "CYCLE CITY"! BUT NOT **US!**

IT'S A TOTAL **NIGHTMARE.**

WELL, THINK OF IT THIS WAY:

YOU'RE YOUNG, YOU'RE HEALTHY, AND THE BIGGEST PROBLEM YOU'VE GOT IS THE NAME OF YOUR BALL TEAM!

GRAMPS IS MINIMIZING MY SUFFERING AGAIN.

AW, TOO BAD, SWEETIE. HAVE A COOKIE.

OPENING DAY, BOYS! OPENING DAY!
LET'S GO GET 'EM!
IS IT TRUE?... IT IS!!
GUYS! THEY REALLY ARE CALLED THE CREAM PUFFS!
HA HA HA HA HA HA
I'M ACTUALLY FEELING NOSTALGIC FOR THE SEASON WE WERE SPONSORED BY "CHEZ LINDA."

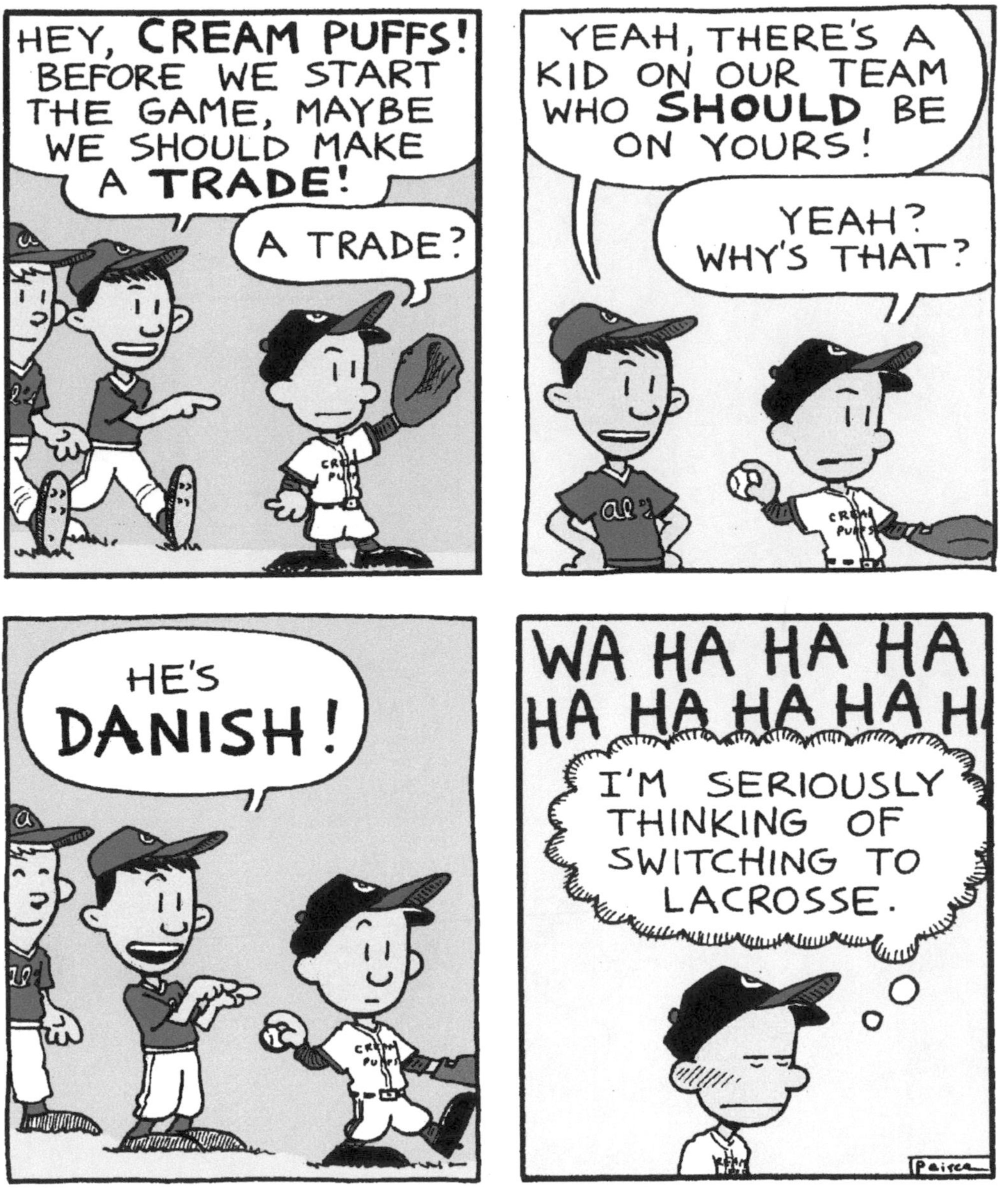
HEY, CREAM PUFFS! BEFORE WE START THE GAME, MAYBE WE SHOULD MAKE A TRADE!
A TRADE?
YEAH, THERE'S A KID ON OUR TEAM WHO SHOULD BE ON YOURS!
YEAH? WHY'S THAT?
HE'S DANISH!
WA HA HA HA HA HA HA HA H
I'M SERIOUSLY THINKING OF SWITCHING TO LACROSSE.
Pairce

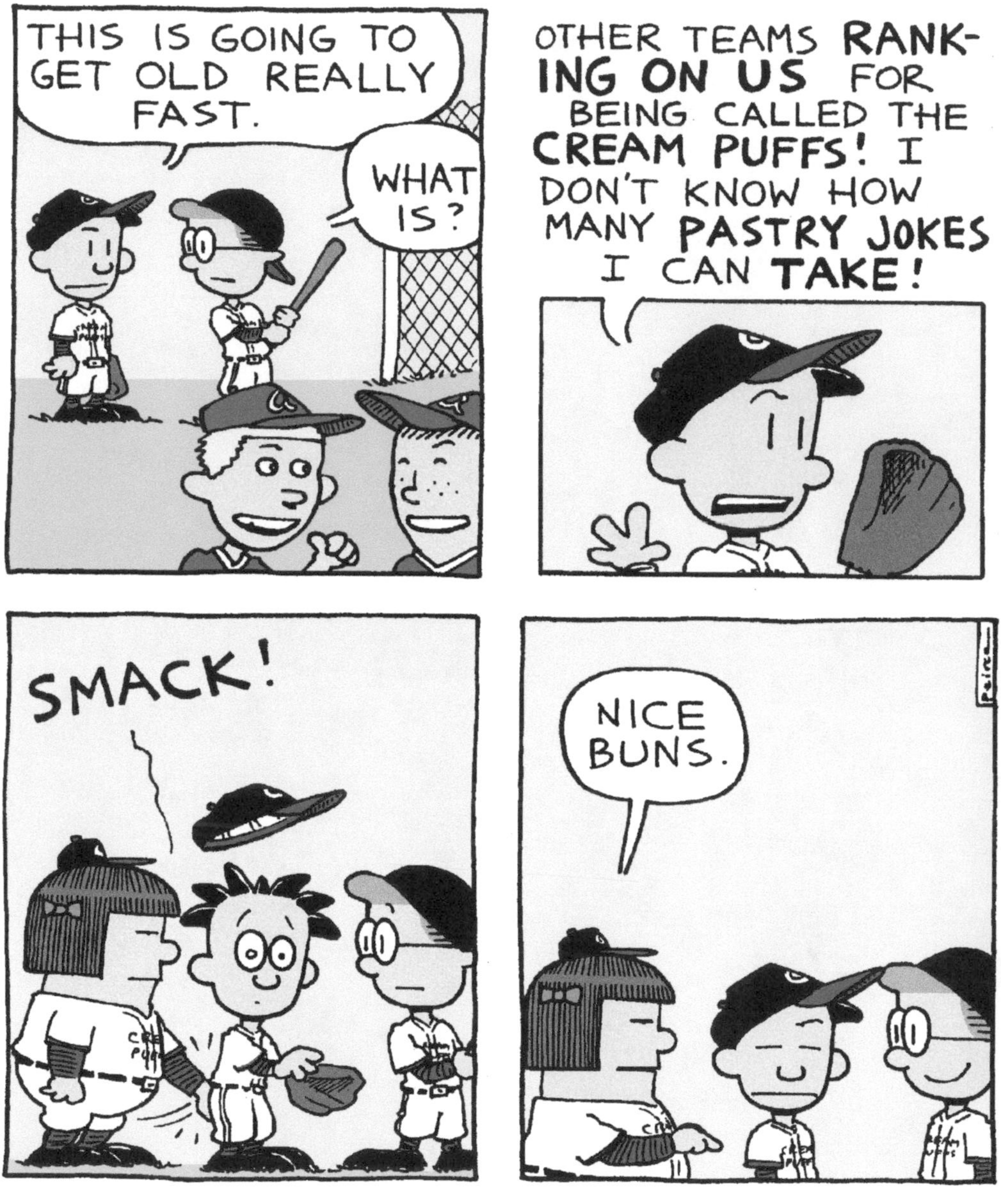
THIS IS GOING TO GET OLD REALLY FAST.
WHAT IS?
OTHER TEAMS RANKING ON US FOR BEING CALLED THE CREAM PUFFS! I DON'T KNOW HOW MANY PASTRY JOKES I CAN TAKE!
SMACK!
NICE BUNS.

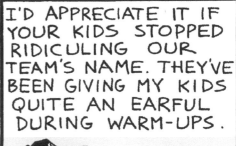

OKAY, GANG, LET'S PLAY BALL! AND IF THE OTHER TEAM WANTS TO MAKE FUN OF OUR NAME, **LET** 'EM!

CLAP CLAP CLAP

WE'LL SHOW 'EM THAT A CREAM PUFF MAY BE... UH... FLAKY ON THE **OUTSIDE**, BUT... IT'S... UM... HM... IT'S...

...SOFT AND SWEET ON THE INSIDE?

TELL YOU WHAT, JUST TAKE THE FIELD.

EPIC FAIL ON THE PRE-GAME PEP TALK, COACH.

WAIT! MRS. GODFREY, YOU CAN'T GIVE US A POP QUIZ! IT'S NOT **FAIR**!

I MEAN, WE DON'T EVEN KNOW WHAT YOU'RE **QUIZZING** US ON! RIGHT, GANG? RIGHT?

WHEN CLASS ENDED YESTERDAY, PEOPLE, WHAT DID I **SPECIFICALLY** ASK YOU TO READ AND REVIEW?

CHAPTER 6, QUESTIONS 12-28!

I HATE THEM ALL.

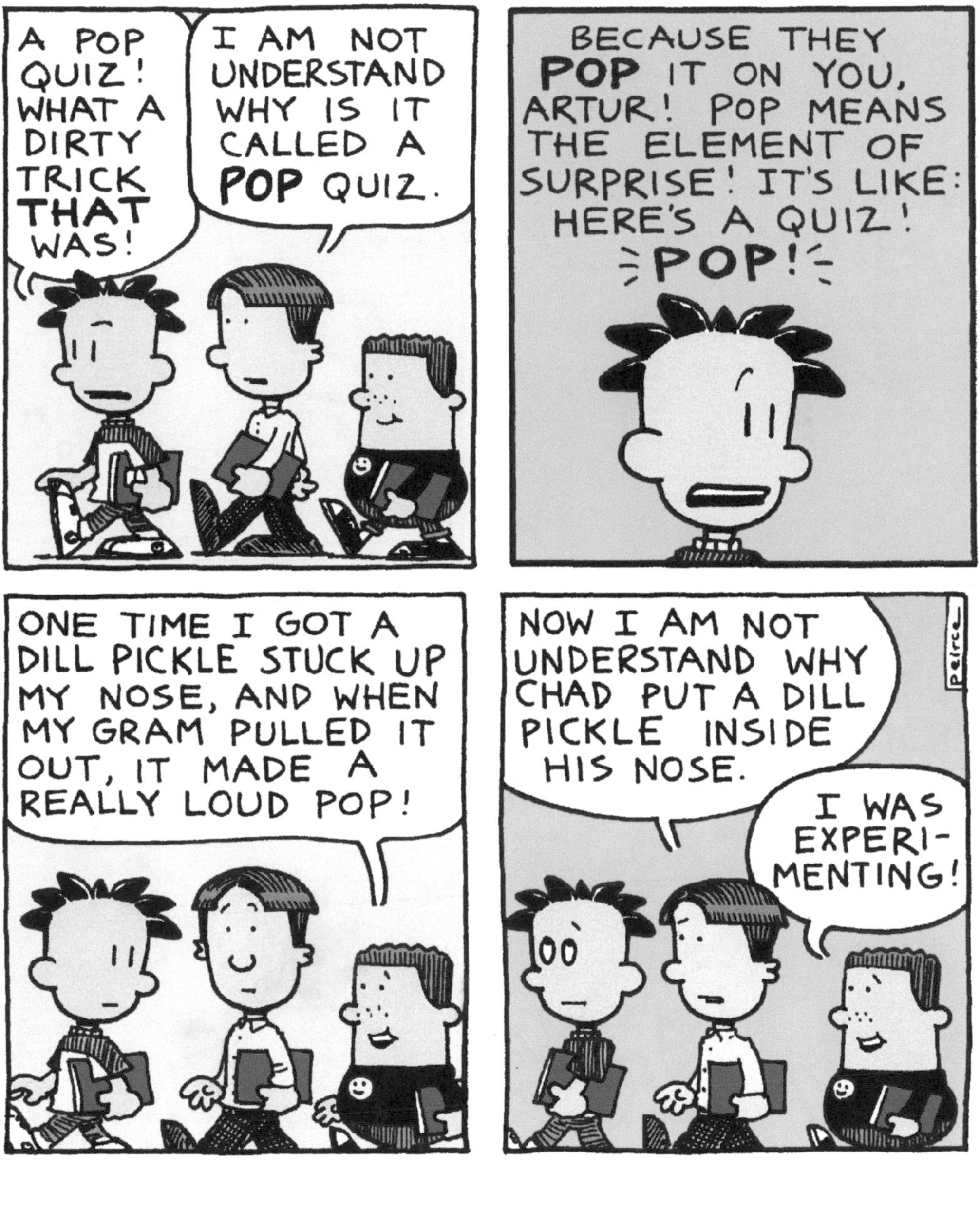
A POP QUIZ! WHAT A DIRTY TRICK THAT WAS!
I AM NOT UNDERSTAND WHY IS IT CALLED A POP QUIZ.
BECAUSE THEY POP IT ON YOU, ARTUR! POP MEANS THE ELEMENT OF SURPRISE! IT'S LIKE: HERE'S A QUIZ! POP!
ONE TIME I GOT A DILL PICKLE STUCK UP MY NOSE, AND WHEN MY GRAM PULLED IT OUT, IT MADE A REALLY LOUD POP!
NOW I AM NOT UNDERSTAND WHY CHAD PUT A DILL PICKLE INSIDE HIS NOSE.
I WAS EXPERI-MENTING!
peirce

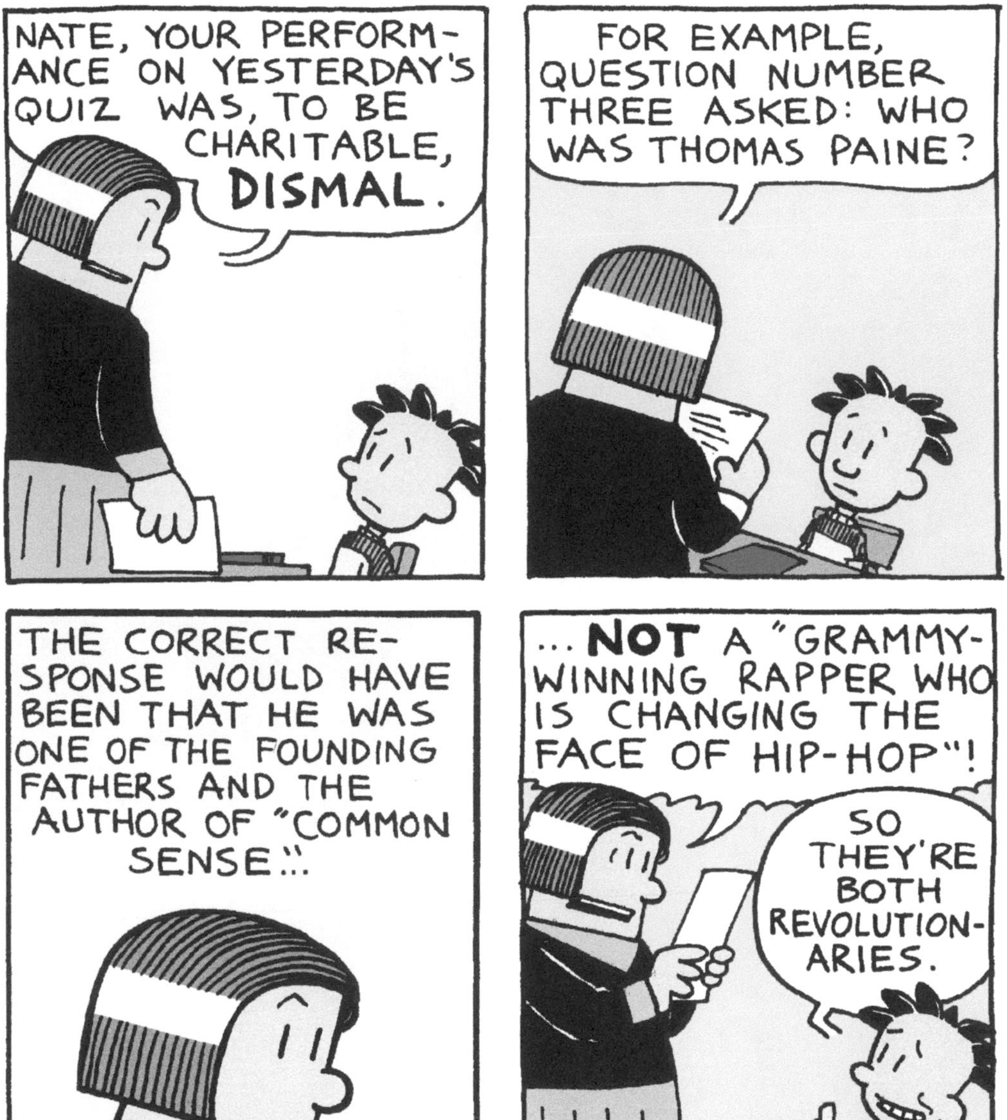
NATE, YOUR PERFORMANCE ON YESTERDAY'S QUIZ WAS, TO BE CHARITABLE, **DISMAL**.
FOR EXAMPLE, QUESTION NUMBER THREE ASKED: WHO WAS THOMAS PAINE?
THE CORRECT RESPONSE WOULD HAVE BEEN THAT HE WAS ONE OF THE FOUNDING FATHERS AND THE AUTHOR OF "COMMON SENSE"...
...**NOT** A "GRAMMY-WINNING RAPPER WHO IS CHANGING THE FACE OF HIP-HOP"!
SO THEY'RE BOTH REVOLUTIONARIES.
Peirce

Andrews McMeel Publishing
a division of Andrews McMeel Universal
1130 Walnut Street, Kansas City, Missouri 64106

www.andrewsmcmeel.com

ISBN: 978-1-4494-7581-9

Library of Congress Control Number: 2015953083

These strips appeared in newspapers from
October 31, 2011, through April 21, 2012.

Big Nate can be viewed on the Internet at
www.gocomics.com/big_nate

ATTENTION: SCHOOLS AND BUSINESSES
Andrews McMeel books are available at quantity discounts with bulk purchase for educational, business, or sales promotional use. For information, please e-mail the Andrews McMeel Publishing Special Sales Department:
specialsales@amuniversal.com.

Check out these and other books at ampkids.com

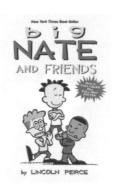

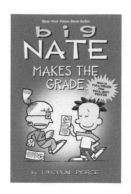

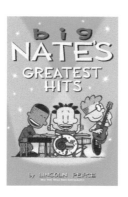

Also available:
Teaching and activity guides for each title.
AMP! Comics for Kids books make reading FUN!

CPSIA information can be obtained
at www.ICGtesting.com
Printed in the USA
LVHW070127100222
710754LV00007B/218